The world need[ed] [someone who] could fight the [...] Jonas Slowman, [...] Shadow," was the best of the best.

Gun in one hand, Emily's hand in the other, Jonas continued his progress along the wooded side of the road in pursuit of a lead. Between his ranger training in the military and his experience with the Brotherhood of Warriors, he knew all the tricks of the trade. But one moment's distraction could result in lethal consequences. Jonas knew how to stay alive, and that's why he was here now instead of in a cemetery on the Navajo Nation. Without focus, he and Emily would be nothing more than the walking dead. That, more than anything, confirmed for him that there was no place for love in his life. It softened a man and muddied his objectivity. And he had to keep Emily safe.

Dear Reader,

Several years ago I began to experience a loss of vision. Those months were without a doubt the most terrifying of my life. Like the heroine, I told no one at first, but eventually David, my husband, guessed what was going on. Throughout that difficult time David stood beside me. It was his love that bolstered my courage whenever it sagged.

For the purposes of this story I've chosen to mirror some of the symptoms I experienced and the issues I confronted, hoping to give you a more intimate glimpse into my life at the time. The terror, the feelings of isolation, the desperate need to plan for the unknown, are all part of my heroine Emily's story, too.

Emily has her project—constructing an inn—to keep her hopes alive. I had my writing. Bringing these stories to you kept me focused and eventually saw me through that period in my life.

I've recovered my sight, but the lessons I learned during those days will remain with me forever. I now know that there's no greater blessing than a love that neither time nor circumstance can stem.

With that in mind, I bring you *The Shadow.*

Aimée Thurlo

AIMÉE
THURLO

THE
SHADOW

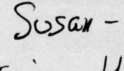

Susan –

Enjoy the
story!

HARLEQUIN®

TORONTO • NEW YORK • LONDON
AMSTERDAM • PARIS • SYDNEY • HAMBURG
STOCKHOLM • ATHENS • TOKYO • MILAN • MADRID
PRAGUE • WARSAW • BUDAPEST • AUCKLAND

To Peg, because between the both of us,
we give new meaning to *mi casa es tu casa*.

And Deb Hetrick who always has something nice to say.

Recycling programs
for this product may
not exist in your area.

ISBN-13: 978-0-373-69448-8

THE SHADOW

Printed in U.S.A.

ABOUT THE AUTHOR

Aimée Thurlo is a nationally known bestselling author. She's the winner of a Career Achievement Award by *RT Book Reviews*, the New Mexico Book Award in contemporary fiction and a Willa Cather Award in the same category. She's published in twenty countries worldwide.

She also cowrites the bestselling Ella Clah mainstream mystery series praised in the *New York Times Book Review*.

Aimée was born in Havana, Cuba, and lives with her husband of thirty-nine years in Corrales, New Mexico. Her husband, David, was raised on the Navajo Indian Reservation.

Books by Aimée Thurlo

HARLEQUIN INTRIGUE
988—COUNCIL OF FIRE*
1011—RESTLESS WIND*
1064—STARGAZER'S WOMAN*
1154—NAVAJO COURAGE*
1181—THE SHADOW*

*Brotherhood of Warriors

Don't miss any of our special offers. Write to us at the following address for information on our newest releases.

Harlequin Reader Service
U.S.: 3010 Walden Ave., P.O. Box 1325, Buffalo, NY 14269
Canadian: P.O. Box 609, Fort Erie, Ont. L2A 5X3

CAST OF CHARACTERS

Jonas Slowman—He had the power to make things happen, but what he wanted most was out of his reach.

Emily Atkins—Her hopes and dreams for the future demanded she stay strong. Yet the warrior who fought beside her was her greatest weakness.

Dinétsoh—The trusted member of the Brotherhood had disappeared with a fortune in bearer bonds that Emily desperately needed.

Robert Jefferson—A real estate lawyer about to make the deal of his life—if he lived long enough to collect.

Grant Woods—He wanted the Atkins property, and wasn't prepared to take no for an answer.

Jen Caldwell—Not so innocent, the legal assistant was in a position to know everything…or so she thought.

Sam Carpenter—He was Grant Woods' handyman, but who was he really working for?

Prologue

Dinétsoh gripped the heavy briefcase tightly with his uninjured hand as he tried to figure out what to do next. He couldn't afford to lose those bearer bonds; anyone could cash them in. The Navajo Nation needed the funds to buy the land where their ancestral refuge had been hidden—then rediscovered, less than ten years ago.

He checked the makeshift bandage on his wounded arm as he stopped behind a tall juniper to catch his breath. The bullet from the high-powered rifle had passed through his arm cleanly, leaving two gaping holes in his biceps. The improvised bandage had temporarily stemmed the flow of blood, but just barely. His head felt light from the loss of blood, and he was running out of time. His strength was fading and he was finding it increasingly difficult to walk, much less run.

Duty drove him now. The Brotherhood of Warriors was counting on him to see this mission through. He'd been their only contact with the Anglo attorney, Powell Atkins. Now he was the only one alive who could identify the person who'd caused the wreck that had killed the attorney, and almost cost Dinétsoh his own life, as well.

Determination kept him moving. He had to live long enough to insure his tribe's future, and the safety of the attorney's daughter. If he failed to survive, the one hunting him would cer-

The Shadow

tainly turn on her next, and the promise the Brotherhood had made her father would be irreparably broken. Only one other Brotherhood Warrior had all the skills to prevent the unthinkable, but there was no way to reach him now.

Dinétsoh suddenly heard a sound in the brush below him. He tightened his grip on the briefcase once more and climbed wearily toward the bluffs. If he couldn't make it to Fire Rock Hollow before dark, all would be lost.

An item fell from his torn pocket onto the sand, but before he could turn to pick it up, he heard the sound of footfalls crunching on the dry ground, coming closer. Ducking behind cover again, he waited. In the fading sunlight, the turquoise key took on a deep green glow. As the tribal artifact fell under a deep shadow, Dinétsoh reluctantly slipped away.

Chapter One

Emily sat in her father's cozy leather chair and leaned back wearily, stretching her muscles. His combination library-office was a total mess. Every inch of the old oak floor was littered with papers, documents and manila folders—a leftover from a burglar's visit two days ago, during her father's funeral. Having learned how to track during her early teens, she'd followed the footprints left by the thief, hoping to find a clue. Unfortunately, the trail had disappeared at the road, replaced by tire tracks. The official police department search had yielded no further answers.

She still had no idea what, if anything, had been taken, except for her father's collection of maps. They'd been in a folder, but she doubted they were of much value.

Emily looked around her. Daylight was only a memory now, and the pair of battery-powered lanterns atop cardboard boxes in two corners of the room were the only sources of illumination. She'd had all the utilities turned off yesterday. The main house, where she was currently, was scheduled to be torn down soon. Though money was tight, she'd given the construction crew the go-ahead, knowing her father would have approved.

Time was her enemy now. Her eyesight was becoming progressively weaker. A month ago she'd been diagnosed with a rare, genetic and progressive form of macular degeneration.

Learning that she was slowly going blind terrified her. A dark wall was descending around her, one that would keep her trapped behind it. Yet the diagnosis, though dire, still held out hope. Recent discoveries in gene therapy hinted that a cure would be found—someday.

After hearing of her condition, her father had encouraged her to quit her job at an Albuquerque area resort and come home. His belief in her had renewed her courage, and with his added financial support, they'd made plans to build a new future—for her and for him.

She missed her father. His passing, in an auto accident, had left a hole inside her. He'd been her only living relative. As she looked around the room, she felt achingly alone.

Suddenly aware that her isolation would make her an easy target if the burglars came back now, she stood. The fading light from one of the battery-powered lanterns was casting long shadows on the wall, and that increased her anxiety.

It was time to go back to the small trailer she'd brought in to serve as her temporary living quarters. Emily slipped out of the main house, locking the door with the knob button by feel. Using her small but powerful flashlight to light the path before her, she picked her way across the grounds.

She was halfway across the yard when she caught the unmistakable scent of gasoline. Shining the beam about, she spotted the vague outline of a person moving around the stack of two-by-sixes the construction crew had left there earlier. She aimed her flashlight at the figure, hoping it was her construction foreman, Ken. As the man turned, she saw that his face was covered with a ski mask.

Emily turned off the light instantly. Taking several quick steps back, she collided with the side of the shed and nearly fell.

The man came toward her with raised arms, holding a board over his head like a big club.

Emily moved to her right, but a second man, also wearing

a mask, suddenly came around the other side of the shed, trapping her between them.

The first man lunged, swinging the board at her head.

Heart hammering in her chest, she ducked under its arc and chopped him on the wrist with her flashlight.

As he yelped and staggered back, she picked up the only close weapon she could find—a cottonwood branch about the length of a yardstick. It was too light to serve as a bludgeon, but it would give her some reach, and she could aim at their faces and target her assailants' eyes.

"What do you want from me?" she demanded, angling her flashlight at the closest man, hoping to blind and confuse him.

He remained silent, but continued to inch forward, shielding his eyes from the glare with a gloved hand.

Without warning, a figure in dark clothes dropped off the roof of the shed, landing beside her in a crouch, like a panther. "Stay put," he whispered.

Turning, the newcomer positioned himself between her and her assailants, and rose to his full height.

Her rescuer's face wasn't masked, but he'd moved too fast for her to get a clear look at him. Grateful for any help, she continued to train the powerful beam of her flashlight on her first assailant, hoping to blind him. From what she could see, her ally's only weapon was the small cylinder he held in his hand—even smaller than her flashlight. Fear pounded through her.

"Back off—while your head's still attached to your shoulders," her rescuer growled.

His voice made her skin prickle. Deadly intent dripped from every syllable.

The closest man automatically took half a step back in response, undoubtedly wondering, like Emily, why anyone holding such a small weapon would show such confidence.

"Walk away while you still can," the first man responded,

coming up. His voice was artificially low, clearly disguised. He didn't have the board now, but his gloved fists were huge.

With a flick of her ally's wrist, the stick in his hand clicked with a low, metallic ring and suddenly became three times as long.

What happened next was a blur. Emily saw her newfound friend rush her closest assailant, and in a heartbeat, that man crashed to the ground. The second one leaped into the fight, but was struck behind the knee and fell face forward.

"Run!" one yelled to his partner. Both men scrambled to their feet and raced away into the brush.

As her rescuer turned around to face her, Emily's mouth went dry and her heart began to pound. Although her night vision was poor, her heart filled in all the small details her eyes were unable to pick up.

"Jonas," she managed to gasp at last. "What are you…?"

He smiled. "Emily. After five years, you still remember?" His voice was smooth and caressing now.

"How could you think I'd ever forget? You saved my life— then, as well as now," she declared, her heart lodged at the back of her throat.

"Get inside, quickly," he urged, collapsing the metal baton and jamming it into his jacket pocket. "I want to take one last look around and make sure nothing here can catch fire. Then you and I need to talk. You're still in danger."

TEN MINUTES LATER, Jonas Slowman sat on a small bench— what was really a storage bin in the trailer—as Emily prepared them something hot to drink. Though it was mid-March and nearly spring, the temperature at night was still in the low forties.

Jonas gazed at her appreciatively. Emily was as beautiful as ever. He pushed back the thought quickly and forced himself to focus. As a member of the Navajo tribe's elite Brotherhood of Warriors, he'd worked many missions, but this promised to be the toughest yet.

Seeing Emily again was more difficult than he'd originally thought. She'd been a part of his dreams since that night on the mountain years ago. He'd stayed away from her for that very reason. But his orders were clear—protect her at all costs—and there was no room for emotions on a mission.

"It's decaf coffee. It's all I've got," she said, turning her head in his direction.

He saw her gaze drift down to his hands, and wondered if seeing his bruised knuckles bothered her. Then, noting the far-away look on her face and the ghost of a shiver that rippled through her, he knew she was remembering the pleasures of his touch. The knowledge bit into him hard.

Finished assembling the four-cup percolator, she came to join him. "Those men…" she began, then took a shaky breath and looked away.

"Are gone and can't hurt you," he said flatly.

"Nothing in my life makes sense anymore—even the fact that we're sitting here face-to-face," she whispered, taking a seat on the folding chair across from him. "I never thought I'd see you again. Over the years, I almost convinced myself that you were a dream."

"I'm not a dream. What we had was real."

He held her gaze, though it cost him. Everything about Emily was made to tempt a man. Dark brown hair spilled over her shoulders, and those soft hazel eyes spoke of gentleness— a quality sadly lacking in his life. But there was more to her than the sum of her parts. The stubborn set of her chin spoke of pride and an independent spirit. And that was the woman he remembered—the one who'd haunted his dreams.

"When the snowstorm ended and you took me back to the lodge, everyone was so excited I'd turned up alive they just closed in around me. I tried to push people back so I could find you again, but you were gone. And I didn't even know your full name. I described you to everyone there, but no one remembered seeing you."

He nodded. Disappearing into the shadows was his specialty. It was a skill he'd learned in the Rangers and had perfected after becoming a member of the Brotherhood of Warriors.

"Once I had a chance to think things through, I understood why you didn't stick around," she continued. "Navajos aren't supposed to show pride, and you didn't seem the kind of man who'd be comfortable getting a million thank-yous. But you never got in touch afterward, not even to say a quick hello."

He heard the trace of disappointment in her voice and, as he met her eyes, felt the tug on his senses. He could still remember every detail of their first meeting—the tiny nylon tent, a woman close to death, one sleeping bag and the heat that brought life.

Yet looking at Emily now, he saw more than the lost girl he'd rescued back then. There was maturity and new strength in her. Clearly, she could handle herself. He'd seen it in the way she'd fought those men, though she'd been armed only with a stick and a flashlight. That had taken guts. To win the fight ahead, all Emily needed was an edge—and that's exactly why he was here.

Seeing the long, thoughtful look she was giving him, he sat back and waited for her to speak.

"After all this time, here you are again, out of nowhere, and right when I need you," she said. She pressed her palm to his heart, and felt it beat against her palm. "You're real."

He placed his hand over hers. "I'm flesh and blood just like you." He heard the small catch in her breath and gave her a thoroughly masculine grin.

She took a step back. "How…why?" she stammered, confused.

"I was sent by the tribe to help you out, and make sure you stay safe. Your father was our friend, and we take care of our own."

"You're a tribal police officer?"

"No, not exactly. But even if I were, this would be out of my jurisdiction. Right now what you need to do is report this incident to the sheriff's department. When you do, give them my Anglo name—Jonas Slowman."

This was the first time she'd heard his full name. He watched her whisper it as if getting a feel for it, and savoring the knowledge. Navajos didn't readily give out their names, which were said to have power an enemy could use against a person. But on her lips, Jonas's name became a caress, a promise.

"I'll be back in a minute. My phone is on the…bed."

As Emily walked down the short passage to pick up the cell phone, he watched her hips sway gently. His body tightened as memories of the past collided with their inescapable present.

Cursing himself, he looked away. The past was gone. This was now and he had a job to do.

EMILY ENDED THE CALL a few minutes later, then returned to sit across the table from him. "They know you at the sheriff's office," she said.

"Some do, some don't. Who did you speak to?"

"A sergeant named Charlie Nez."

Jonas nodded. "He's Navajo. We went to Shiprock High together…back in the stagecoach and wagon train days."

She laughed. He was trying to get her to relax and it was working. "They said they'd send out a deputy later to take our statements—long distances, and not so many officers, I guess."

Emily sipped her coffee. Her pulse had slowed to a normal rate, and now that she could think clearly, she knew there was more to Jonas's visit than he'd told her. He hadn't just shown up—he'd been watching her property. But for how long?

Minutes of silence stretched out between them as questions circled in her mind. Tired of waiting for him to fill in the gaps, she decided to probe for answers. "My father had many clients, and he never discussed their business with me, but I get the impression that the work he did for the tribe had many layers."

She allowed what she hadn't said to linger between them. Working as an innkeeper at a mountain resort east of Albuquerque had taught her that people often talked to hear the sound of their own voices, or to make sure their opinions still mattered. All you had to do was be willing to wait, and listen.

Yet rules didn't seem to apply to Jonas Slowman. When her patience finally stretched to the limit, she continued. "Was it me you were watching, or the men who attacked me? Just exactly what kind of work do you do for the tribe?"

Jonas leaned back in his seat and regarded her for a moment. "I'm what's best described as a vindicator—one who defends a cause—at least that's the English equivalent. My work enables the tribe to continue to walk in beauty."

"How does that connect to my dad?"

"Your father handled some delicate matters for our tribe. The circumstances surrounding his death have raised some questions for us, and I was sent to provide any help you might need."

She sat up abruptly. "Are you telling me that the tribe doesn't think that what happened to Dad was just an accident?"

Jonas remained quiet for several long moments. "We have no proof to the contrary, but questions remain. For example, your father was the last person to see one of our people—a man who's now missing. We believe he may have been in your dad's car when it crashed."

"You mean, somebody wandered off badly hurt and is out there somewhere?"

"A search was conducted the day and night following the accident, and is still going on, but there's been no sign of him. He may have caught a ride along the highway—or not. So far, we have nothing to go on."

"Who's the missing man? Anyone I know?"

"The tribe has its own reasons for wanting to keep his identity a secret for now."

"But the tribe thinks his disappearance might somehow be connected to what happened to Dad?"

"The timing and other factors fit," Jonas said with a nod. "If we're right, and your father's death *wasn't* an accident, you can use someone like me around. I'm here to offer my services."

His unwavering gaze nearly tore her breath away, but she kept her wits about her. "I obviously need some form of security, but I can't afford it right now. My funds are tied into the new construction. Dad and I were getting ready to build a vacation inn for people with special needs. But some of the funds we were expecting haven't come in yet, so I'm living on a very tight budget."

"No payment's necessary. I've got you covered," he said.

Seeing herself reflected in those intense dark eyes brought back a kaleidoscope of emotions that left her feeling weak at the knees. Sharing his sleeping bag…and what had happened next…had kept her from dying of hypothermia. But maybe what they'd shared hadn't meant the same to him. For all she knew, he saw it as nothing more than an unusual one-nighter.

The fact was she *didn't* know, and maybe it was better that way. She needed to take him at face value now and stop looking back. Five years was a very long time. Jonas didn't have a ring on his finger, but he'd obviously gone on with his life.

"I can't pay you, Jonas," she said at last, "but I have something to offer. I'd be happy to search the property, talk to my neighbors and do whatever else you might need to find the missing man."

"There's balance in what you propose," he said. "I accept your arrangement."

"Is the missing man a vindicator like you?"

He shook his head. "His service to the tribe goes above and beyond what I do."

"It would help if I could view a photo. I'd be happy to keep everything confidential."

"I'll see if I can get you one," he said.

As she looked up at him, her heart skipped a beat. His face was chiseled and his expression as hard as steel—but it could be gentle, too, at the right moments. Though that was based on her memory of the past, she could see echoes of it in the coal-black eyes that held hers.

Jonas was a walking temptation, his body lean and hard. Judging from the way he could fight, he was also the most dangerous man she'd ever met. He was like a strong wind that swept away everything in its path. But she needed more in her life than another unforgettable adventure. Her future depended on every decision she made, or failed to make, now.

Wanting to put some distance between them, she began wiping down the counter, though it was perfectly clean.

"What's on your mind? Are you already having second thoughts about our deal?" he pressed.

The fact that he could read her so easily startled her, but she rebounded quickly and did her best to cover. "If you're right, I'm caught in something I just don't understand, except that it seems connected to my dad and this place. But that's not much to go on." She swallowed hard. "I'm not a coward, but it's hard to fight an enemy when you have no idea who that person is, and why he or she is after you."

"That's why I'm here—to equalize the odds."

His voice was filled with an assurance and confidence that was contagious. "Welcome aboard then." She smiled and reached out, offering to shake hands. Then, remembering Navajos didn't believe in casual touch, she drew back. "Sorry."

Jonas reached for her hand and shook it. "You and I are hardly strangers."

A vivid image of her lying naked in his arms, their bodies pressed tightly together, flashed in her mind. The cold surrounding them had given way to heat….

"You and I will start fresh today," she said firmly, mostly for her own benefit. "History is only for those who like to live in the past." Yet even as she spoke, she found it impossible not to notice the strength he kept in check or the hardness of his calloused palm. Though her insides were doing somersaults, she gave him an easy smile.

"I'm here to do a job. And believe me when I tell you that I'm very good at what I do." His voice was calm, yet had an unmistakable edge that caught her attention and held it. "You've never been safer."

The timbre of his voice sent a thrill up her spine. Jonas was the stuff dreams were made of. Somewhere along the way, he'd also acquired a quiet confidence that enhanced everything about him, and teased her imagination.

Emily turned and poured herself another cup of coffee. She wasn't just losing her sight, she was losing what was left of her mind. She had more problems now than she knew what to do with. The last thing she needed was another complication.

Jonas was a temporary ally—that was all. As experience had repeatedly taught her, wishes were only the fragile whispers of a lonely heart.

Chapter Two

Shortly after eight the following morning, Emily noticed a patrol car in the distance motoring slowly down the highway.

The deputies had told her last night when they'd come to take Jonas's and her statements that they'd be increasing Jonas's presence in the area.

Standing at the sink of the trailer, Emily watched the main house from the small window. Jonas had insisted on sleeping outside. He'd parked his truck in a spot that allowed him to keep watch on her trailer, the construction materials and the main house.

His presence reassured her even more than the added sheriff's department deputies on patrol. Yet even so, she hadn't been able to get much sleep last night. Thoughts and worries had chased each other in an endless circle.

The news that her father might have been murdered had turned her world upside down. No matter how she looked at it, her life was now a maze of uncertainty filled with what-ifs.

Emily took two mugs of coffee from the counter and stepped out of the trailer, trying to ignore the cold wind whipping against her. Halfway across the grounds, she glanced at the ten-by-twelve-foot concrete pad that had once been intended as a floor for her mother's hobby room.

Her mom had vanished the day before it was poured, thirteen years ago, and the structure had never gone beyond that first step. Emily's dad had always believed that her mom would someday return, so he'd left it there, ready for completion when the time came. But her mom hadn't come home. Eventually, the police had stopped searching for answers. As the years went by, her dad, too, had come to terms with their loss.

Old doubts filled Emily's mind as she thought about her mother. As a kid she'd spend many nights wondering if she'd somehow been the reason her mom had left.

Taking a deep breath, she stopped those musings abruptly. Her mother had made her choice. Now new dreams would spring up where the old had been. That useless concrete pad would be replaced by a new foundation. Once the Tamarisk Inn was up and running, Emily would build her own private residence on that spot.

As she reached the main house, she found Jonas by the back door, waiting. He was wearing low-slung jeans and a flannel shirt that fitted his wide shoulders snugly.

"Good morning," she called, and held up the mugs. "I brought a cup for you, too."

"Caffeinated?" he asked, sounding decidedly hopeful.

"Nope. Never drink the stuff. It gives me the jitters."

"Then I guess this'll have to do," he answered with a martyred sigh. "Did you eat breakfast already?"

"I had a piece of toast. I don't generally have breakfast." Feeling guilty when she realized he was probably hungry, she added, "But my fridge is full. Help yourself to whatever you'd like. I've got plenty of eggs, bread and milk."

"Thanks, but I'll wait," he answered, and followed her inside the house.

The interior felt bitterly cold. Standing on a step stool, she lifted off the curtain rod and removed the drapes from one window. The morning light immediately spilled inside. Emily knew a wave of warmth would soon be flowing across the room.

Not realizing Jonas was behind her, she stepped down from

the stool, turned around with the curtains still in hand and ran right into his rock-hard chest. Her heart did a crazy somersault and awareness made her tingle all the way to her toes.

"Excuse me," she muttered as he steadied her.

With a smile hovering around the corners of his mouth, he stepped aside.

Avoiding his gaze, she moved from window to window, taking down the remaining curtains and folding them. She then packed them into cardboard boxes, trying her best to avoid looking at Jonas. He was leaning in the doorway, arms and ankles crossed.

"Was last night the first time you had trouble with intruders?" he asked.

"No," she said, and explained about the break-in the day of her father's funeral and the missing maps. "They were of different quadrants here on our land, but not particularly valuable."

He remembered his briefing. Diné Nééz, his contact, had raised the possibility that Dinétsoh might have gone to Fire Rock Hollow, the historical refuge legendary warriors like Manuelito had once used.

Its location had been lost for nearly a century. Then one day, the attorney had found the turquoise key near some ruins on his property. He'd showed it to Dinétsoh, his friend and associate, and together they'd rediscovered the place.

After that, Dinétsoh, appointed the cave's new guardian, had kept the key with him, and to honor the past, had stocked the refuge with provisions. At the time of the accident, Dinétsoh and Powell Atkins had been on their way to conclude the sale that would have given the tribe ownership of that parcel of land.

"How will you deal with your father's papers?" Jonas asked, glancing into what had been Powell Atkins's office.

"I don't have time to do much sorting, so I'm placing everything in storage. If there's anything in there that pertains to the tribe, you're welcome to it. Dad also had some papers in his safe-deposit box in town. I haven't looked through those yet, except to get a few documents I needed right away, like his will, tax forms and the mortgage papers."

"You should go through everything he placed in the bank as soon as possible. You might find some answers there," Jonas advised, entering the office and glancing around. It was possible that Emily's father had hidden something others wanted badly enough to kill for.

Emily stood by a window, gazing at the row of stacked lumber and construction materials opposite the house. "I think those men last night were trying to burn me out, beginning with my building materials."

"Losing all that lumber and sheeting would have cost you thousands of dollars."

"It would have been a disaster," she agreed in a whisper. "I honestly don't know if I could have recovered from a loss like that. My insurance rates would have doubled or tripled, and replacing the materials would have been extremely costly. Everything's gone up so much lately."

"You should consider going away for a while and staying someplace safe—at least until we can figure out what you're up against." As he glanced at Emily, Jonas saw her back straighten and her chin jut out in defiance. "It was just a suggestion."

"No one's going to chase me away," she declared, facing him squarely. Then she exhaled softly and in a whisper added, "Life's not taking anything else away from me—not without a fight."

The last part obviously hadn't been meant for his ears, but the haunting sense of isolation that had resonated in her words touched him deeply. His thoughts drifted back to an afternoon at an Afghan border village and the few hours that had changed him forever. One moment's distraction, a suicide bomber, then bodies everywhere.

He'd sworn back then never to lower his guard again. Life was about survival, and to do that, you had to fight to stay in control—of yourself and your situation. That required constant vigilance and a fighting spirit that refused surrender—a spirit like Emily's.

"Just hang tough, Em. I'll help you finish what you've set out to do." His words carried the power of authority and utter conviction.

"Don't make promises you may not be able to keep," she retorted.

"I get things done. You can count on that." As she glanced up at him he saw the flicker in her eyes, and recognized the return of hope. "I need to go meet someone, but I'll be back soon."

"Take your time. I'll be fine. It's broad daylight. What can happen?"

He didn't answer. Jonas gave her one last look as she sat beneath the open window, placing papers into folders, then packing them into boxes.

Something else about Emily had changed. There was a quiet dignity about her that was new, and it intrigued him. He'd seen much the same look on the faces of fellow Rangers going into battle. He wasn't sure how that fit yet, but it was that same quiet courage he saw in Emily now.

JONAS DROVE TO A HILLOCK halfway to the highway, where cell phone reception would be stronger, and privacy insured. He had no doubt that last night's incident would already be known to Diné Nééz. The man had contacts everywhere in the Four Corners and there was little he missed.

He climbed out of his pickup and walked into the *bosque,* as the wooded area was called, stopping beside a thicket of salt cedars. Before he'd even finished dialing, Jonas felt it—a wave of movement in the air.

He bent at the knees, automatically making himself a smaller target as he turned. Just then he saw Diné Nééz appear from behind an old cottonweed tree scarred by age and the elements.

The middle-aged Navajo nodded to Jonas, and gestured for him to put away the phone. There was no need for it now. "We've had someone watching since the report to the police came in last night. The tracks left by the two men ended near the highway, so there's not much I can offer you on that, but if you run into more trouble than you can handle, call. Backup will be twenty minutes away or less."

"My priority remains the woman?"

"Yes. We're handling the search for Dinétsoh. But if you come across something that reveals his whereabouts, pursue the lead."

"Those men weren't there just to set fires. I think they were coming for her. She either knows something that she's not aware of, or is an obstruction to whatever plan they have."

"It's also possible that others are searching for Dinétsoh, and last night's events were just a diversion," Diné Nééz said.

"Has word gotten out about the bearer bonds?" Jonas asked quickly.

"No. We've managed to keep a lid on that, at least for now. But there's no telling how long that'll last. One slip is all it takes." He gathered his thoughts before continuing. "The woman… In your opinion, will she be an asset or a liability to our search?"

Jonas considered his answer carefully. "She's offered to help, and give me access to her land. But she has secrets, too. I can feel it in my gut."

"Don't we all?" the man countered with a shrug. "Is it possible that whatever she's hiding has something to do with her father's death?"

"I can't be certain of anything at this point." *Except for one thing,* Jonas added silently. His attraction to her hadn't diminished. If anything, it had grown even stronger. And that would make him a liability to the mission unless he kept it in check. "I'll report as soon as I have something."

"We need to put the case together quickly, but our involvement has to be kept under wraps. The Brotherhood has remained a secret organization since the time of Kit Carson—unseen but felt—and that's how it must remain. Live up to your code name, *Chaha'oh*," he said. It was the Navajo word for *shadow*. "Use your skills and get it done."

JONAS RETURNED TO THE house and parked next to it. As he stepped out of the cab, the hairs on the back of his neck stood on end. Something wasn't right. Remaining beside the truck, he waited and listened, trying to pinpoint what was bothering him. This same instinct had kept him alive more times than he cared to count, and taught him to pay attention to subtleties.

He watched the play of light and shadows on the ground, and somewhere in the distance heard the sound of soft humming. As he walked around the house, he saw Emily standing outside the back door, her eyes closed, her face tilted up toward the sky.

For a moment he just gazed at her, absorbing the way her brown hair cascaded around her shoulders as she enjoyed the warmth. The last time he'd seen her look that serene and happy they'd just made love. Safely nestled against him inside his sleeping bag, she'd looked up at him and smiled. That moment in time had been permanently carved into his heart.

Tearing his gaze away, he muttered an oath. Diversions and distractions were an implacable enemy, and danger *was* close. He wasn't sure how he knew, but he felt it as clearly as the cool breeze that penetrated his open leather jacket.

Darting his eyes around, he joined her quickly. "Let's go inside," he said, forcing his voice to remain casual. "Maybe I can help you finish emptying the rooms."

"You weren't gone long," she answered pleasantly.

"I just needed to check in with a few people and see if anything new had turned up on our missing man."

"And has it?"

He shook his head.

She led him through the kitchen, returning to what had been her father's office. "I've gone through all the files Dad kept here. His maps are missing, as I told you, though the folder was still in the cabinet. Nothing else seemed out of the ordinary. I also didn't see anything that pertained specifically to the tribe, so I stopped trying to sort and just stuck everything in those boxes. They'll go into storage alongside the furniture."

Hearing a truck engine, she looked out the window and smiled. "Finally! Here are the movers. They'll load the rest of the big stuff into the truck and haul it over to the rental storage place in town."

Still uneasy but unable to identify the threat, Jonas walked out with her and remained by her side while the workers loaded the truck. As soon as they drove off, he and Emily returned inside the house.

"I've never heard of that moving company," he said. "I assume you checked them out?"

"Of course. They're new, but legit, and they gave me a great price. I've got to cut corners now. Every dollar counts."

She hadn't asked for, nor did she want, his sympathy. She'd simply stated a fact. His admiration for her continued to grow.

He looked around the interior, noting that nothing except portable lanterns and labeled boxes remained.

"Everything else in here will be transferred across the driveway to that railroad-car-size metal storage container," she said.

"Since the bulk of the work is finally done, how about you and me taking a break? There's a real nice coffeehouse out on east Main, at the mall. They serve the best pancakes for miles. We can have a quick brunch, then get back to work."

"Great idea," she said, walking outside with him.

Jonas studied the area around him carefully. Someone was out there. He could feel him. As it had been when snipers had stalked his unit, his muscles were wound tight, and he was ready—itching, really—for a challenge.

They were several feet from his truck when he saw a flicker of movement to his left, between two stacks of plywood. Jonas urged Emily quickly into his truck and, motioning for her to stay down, made his way toward the intruder, creeping silently in his soft deerskin boots.

The man never heard or saw him coming. As soon as he was within a few yards, Jonas dived for him, but only caught the heel of his shoe. The intruder, dressed in green coveralls and a cap, dropped something as he kicked loose, then took off at breakneck speed, rounding the corner.

Jonas raced across the yard after him, but before he could narrow the distance, he heard a small motor revving up somewhere ahead. Suddenly a dirt bike roared around the side of the house, raising a cloud of dust as it accelerated straight at him.

Two men. He should have expected it. Jonas automatically reached for the holstered Beretta at the small of his back, then changed his mind. He needed a prisoner, not another casualty. There was a better way to unseat this guy, but his timing would have to be perfect.

Jonas crouched slightly, wondering if his baton would do the trick, then decided it was too light. His forearm was the best choice, though the risk of collision and broken bones was greater. He waved the cyclist forward, goading him with a look of defiance.

The rider, his features hidden by a helmet, didn't waver for a second. He came right at him, engine roaring.

Jonas jumped clear at the last second, throwing out his arm to clothesline the punk. But fate wasn't on his side. The bike suddenly fishtailed, and the rear wheel whipped around. The rider's boot caught him in the shin, spinning Jonas out of position. His fist ricocheted off the top of the biker's helmet as he passed.

The man raced away, fishtailing again about fifty feet farther down the road, then disappearing in the direction of the highway.

His leg throbbing with pain and his fist numb, Jonas tried to locate the man who'd run off on foot. He was out of sight now, and probably making a beeline for his partner on the bike.

Jonas sprinted after the cycle, suspecting the biker would have to stop soon to pick up his cohort. After running another fifty yards, Jonas spotted the bike through the trees, and saw the second man jump behind the driver. As the motorcycle raced off in a cloud of dust, Jonas knew he'd never catch them now, even if he went back for his truck.

Coming to a stop, he opened his cell phone and punched out the number of his contact in the sheriff's department, Sergeant Charlie Nez. Charlie's code name was Ha'asídí, Watchman. After identifying himself and giving him the highlights of the incident, Jonas returned the phone to his jacket pocket and jogged back toward the house.

He was picking up the object his first attacker had dropped—a Taser—when he heard running footsteps. Just then Emily came around the eight-foot-high stack of sheeting, a double-barreled shotgun gripped in her hand.

"They're gone," he assured her quickly.

"What about you? Are you all right?" she asked. "I called the sheriff's department and they said they were sending a deputy."

"I called them, too," he said, noting that she'd wrapped her fingers around the trigger guard. If it was loaded, and the safety off… "Do you know how to use that?"

She looked down at the weapon, then drew it closer, fortunately moving her grip away from the trigger area. "How hard can it be? Point and shoot."

He gently took the weapon from her hands and thumbed the safety on. "Nice. Remington over/under. Where did you get it?"

"It belonged to my dad. He used to go duck hunting. I took

it to my trailer a few days ago, just for safety's sake. I don't really know if it's loaded or not," she added. "I'm not sure how to check. The gun was always off-limits to Mom and me."

Jonas opened the action and checked. "It isn't loaded," he answered. "What were you planning to do if it wouldn't fire?"

"It's nice and heavy. I'd use it as a club."

"To protect me?" he asked, doing his best, but not quite succeeding to bite back a smile.

"Of course. Anyone who got whacked on the head with this would be out of it for a while."

He took a step closer to her, then brushed a stray lock of hair away from her eyes. Hearing her draw in an unsteady breath, he felt a surge of pure masculine satisfaction.

Emily moved away and cleared her throat. "We've had two vandalism attempts here in the past twenty-four hours. What's going on? The bad guys don't normally come back to a crime scene, do they?"

"It depends on how serious they are about putting you out of business."

"But why? An inn brings visitors and more business to the community. This doesn't make sense. Were the men who came today the same ones who were here last night?"

"Probably. The boot and shoe prints match, and the body types fit, at least with height and build." He glanced down at the Taser, studying it. "This was meant to incapacitate me, and maybe you, as well, while they did whatever it was they came for."

"Vandalism wasn't their only objective today. They want to scare me into leaving," she said flatly. "Otherwise, they would have waited until I'd left on an errand, and wouldn't have brought a Taser along."

"I agree. Like last night, scaring you was one of their objectives. If they'd wanted to kill either one of us, they'd have come better armed." He paused for several moments, looking for anything on the Taser that might give them a clue. The serial numbers had been removed, and the insulated grip probably meant no fingerprints could be recovered.

"Do you think they'll try again?" With effort she kept her voice steady.

"Yeah," Jonas grunted. "That's why you should reconsider your plans. Since construction hasn't started yet, why don't you return what materials you can, take a small loss, then wait them out? Give me time to work. Afterward, when things are settled, you can continue."

"No, the clock's ticking too fast—" She abruptly stopped speaking.

"We're on the same side, Em. Don't shut me out," he said, more convinced than ever that she was hiding something. Turning to face her, he took her hand and brought it to his lips. "I've earned your trust many times over. Talk to me."

As she looked into his eyes, her thoughts suddenly became muddled and her heart began doing flip-flops. Forcing a steadiness she wouldn't have thought possible into her voice, she answered him. "I'd like to trust you completely, Jonas. I really would. But here's the thing. I never thought I'd see you again. Then, out of nowhere, here you are."

She paused, pushing her hands deep inside her jacket pockets so she wouldn't be tempted to reach out and touch him. "Though you've saved my life twice, something tells me there's more to your return into my life than you've said. Until I know enough to fill in all those blanks, there's no room for total trust."

"No one can ever fill in all the blanks of another person's life. Things just don't work that way." He leaned against the house, thumbs hooked into the belt loops of his jeans. "You need to make some decisions, and here's something you should consider. Your father spent a lifetime working for the tribe. He trusted us. Can you afford to do anything less?"

"Life's been…different to me. It's taught me to be cautious."

Jonas couldn't fault her for that. In that one way, they were alike.

"But you're right. Once these people realize I won't run away, they're going to come after me with everything they've got."

"No one's going to hurt you, Em." He brushed her cheek with the palm of his hand and felt the gentle tremor that traveled through her. "I'll be right there with you every step of the way."

Chapter Three

Emily sat in what had been the living room of her parent's house. Across the card table from her, in a metal folding chair identical to her own, sat uniformed deputy Michael Dusenberry. Sergeant Nez, whom she'd spoken to earlier on the phone, was questioning Jonas in a separate room.

"How do you explain what's happened?" Deputy Dusenberry asked. "This is the second time vandals have come onto your property. Do you have any idea what they're after?"

"I honestly don't know. They haven't made any attempt to steal my old Chevy, and there's nothing exceptionally valuable here at the house. My dad made a good living, but he wasn't wealthy. All the tools, furniture and appliances are well used and out of sight now, locked up in a metal storage building."

"Have they targeted anything special?"

"The lumber and other building materials, but I don't see what they'd have to gain from setting it all on fire."

"Yet they've come back twice. There's got to be something they want. What about your father's papers and files? As a lawyer he has made his share of enemies."

"I've gone through most of his files looking for something that could be triggering these attacks on me, but so far I haven't found anything," she said, filling in the details. "The only thing missing is my dad's map collection, and that's not worth much. That's all they took."

"Are you sure about that? And if you are, is it possible your father threw the maps out and never got around to discarding the folder from the filing cabinet?"

"The maps were nothing special," she assured him. "And Dad was a neat freak when it came to his files. He would have discarded both folder or maps, or neither."

"I'd ask you to turn all your father's records over to us to sort through, but the truth is we can't fund the man-hours when no major crimes have been committed. It's a matter of priorities and resources."

"I couldn't have turned them over to you anyway—not without a court order. My dad protected his clients' confidentiality, and I'd have to respect that, too."

"Admirable, but if you feel threatened, I'd advise you to hire a trained expert to examine those files for possible suspects."

She shook her head. "I can't. My money situation is similar to your department's."

Jonas walked into the room just then, and the sergeant who'd questioned him followed.

Jonas glanced at Charlie, then back at Emily. "Take things one step at a time, Em. You'll get further that way."

"I'm done here," Deputy Dusenberry said, standing up and placing his notebook in a shirt pocket.

"If you need us, just call," Sergeant Nez added.

Emily saw the officers to the door, spoke briefly to the reporter outside, then excused herself and returned to the house.

Standing by the window, she watched them drive away. "It's such a beautiful day. I wish there wasn't so much to do here."

Jonas gently pulled her toward him and away from the window. "It's not a good idea to stand in front of the glass like that."

Although his words reminded her of the seriousness of the

situation, the warmth of his body crept around her, awakening needs.

"I'm going to take a look outside," he said, moving away. "I'll be back."

She watched him go, noting the tension that tightened his muscles. An edge of danger defined Jonas. It was there in his long-legged stride and the grim set of his rock-hard jaw. Though he'd chosen a path in life that was wildly different from hers, it seemed to suit him perfectly. Like the wind, he'd be here one day, gone the next.

Her inn, on the other hand, would be a part of her life forever. If she could keep her priorities straight, she'd be just fine.

Jonas returned inside moments later and helped her remove a light fixture from the wall. "We've been working under the assumption that someone's threatening you because of something your father was involved in," he said. "But is it possible you've made enemies, too?"

"I don't see how that's possible. I've only been back a few days," she answered, surprised by his question.

"What about enemies from your past—old boyfriends, neighbors, people from work who think you've offended them, or a stalker who followed you here from Albuquerque?"

"I lived in the city and worked at a mountain resort. I got along with my boss and fellow employees, kept my distance from the clients and barely knew my neighbors." She shook her head. "If I'd had any enemies, I would have known long before I moved back here."

"You failed to mention boyfriends," Jonas pointed out.

"A few along the way, but nobody for long. And the break-ups were all amicable."

"At least you think they were. Ever get any strange, or pushy e-mails, phone calls? Have you noticed any strange people hanging around your…apartment?"

"Nope, just a gray cat. After about a week, his owner tracked him down. Sorry, but I can't think of anyone."

"That's okay. So who have you seen and spoken to since you moved back?" he pressed, undaunted.

"Starting close to home, there's my neighbor, Grant Woods. I've known him since high school. He came over to give me his condolences." She paused. "He also expressed an interest in buying all my land. He comes from a wealthy family and is always looking for investments. He figured I wouldn't be staying. After I told him about my plans for the inn, we didn't talk about it anymore," she said. "I also got some other offers—one from a developer and another from one of the utility companies. They wanted drilling and mineral rights."

"There's nothing unusual about any of those offers. Land sells quickly around here. This area's rich with natural gas and that makes it a potential bonanza for an investor. But none of that explains the men after you."

"Maybe someone's hoping to scare me, so I'll sell out." She shook her head. "That doesn't make sense, either. There are multiple bidders. I could sell to whoever I wanted. There's no way any of them could insure they'd be the new owner. And why help out the competition?"

"All right. Let's set that aside for now and finish in here. What's next?" he asked.

"I want to remove all the hardware and a few built-ins, like the fireplace mantel. Whatever stays will be demolished along with the house, and that's scheduled to begin tomorrow."

"Where do you want to put this stuff?"

"In that big metal storage compartment over there." She pointed to the green, metal bin beside the driveway, across from her trailer. "It'll be pretty full after that, but I can't afford any additional storage places, so the boxes over there with dishes and housewares will go to my dad's workshop. It's that small building on the south side of the house."

"What kind of workshop?"

"Dad liked tinkering with wood. Spending hours there was his way of relaxing." And hiding out. After her mother's disappearance, he'd spent most of his free time there—away from her.

Emily pointed toward the den. "The boxes in there marked with a red *D* for donation are going to charity. They're filled with Dad's belongings," she added, her voice wavering slightly.

"You okay?" he murmured, eyeing her closely.

She nodded. "Packing those was very hard."

"Your dad's clothing?" he asked, taking a few steps toward the boxes.

She nodded again. "If you know anyone who might be able to use them…"

"No," he answered quickly. "The People have taboos against that."

"Sorry. I forgot," she said. "Something to do with ghosts. Is that right?"

"No, not ghosts—not exactly, anyway," he stated. "Navajos believe that the good in a man merges with universal harmony, but the *chindi*, the evil side, remains earthbound, ready to create problems for the living. The *chindi* is said to be particularly attached to a person's earthly possessions, so Navajos avoid coming into contact with those."

"All right then," she said with a nod. "Dad's clothes will go to the homeless shelter as planned."

"Did you search his clothes carefully? People often forget what they've stuck in their pockets."

"I thought of that, but didn't find anything." She sighed. "Dad wasn't the careless type. He was methodical and careful. But I'm making him sound too serious, and that's way off the mark. Dad loved games."

"What kind of games?"

"The kind that offered a challenge, and a high degree of intelligence to solve. For example, he refused to have a safe in the house because he said safes could be stolen. If he had something of particular importance to him, and it wasn't related to business, he'd just hide it. He loved mind games. He told me that a thief would have to know him personally to even get close to something he'd hidden."

She laughed softly. "One summer he hid an Ella Clah mystery I'd been reading. It took me two weeks to track it down. He'd placed it on the top of our grandfather clock behind the crown. You had to be eight feet tall or up on a ladder to spot it."

"Now he's left you with another puzzle to solve," Jonas commented thoughtfully.

She nodded. "Guessing what he was into."

THEY WORKED TOGETHER for two hours, then started taking boxes to the workshop. After the third load, as they stopped to take a break, they heard the sound of an approaching vehicle.

Jonas went to the workshop's double doors and studied the truck coming toward them. "Know anyone in a tan crew cab pickup?"

"Not that I can think of offhand," she answered, coming to join him. "My foreman, Ken, drives a big white truck with his company logo on the door."

Without making a point of it, Jonas stepped in front of her. The gesture reminded her of the danger she was facing, but at the same time his protectiveness was reassuring.

Moments later a man in jeans, a windbreaker, boots and a brown baseball cap climbed out of the truck.

Emily breathed a sigh of relief. "That's my neighbor, Grant Woods," she said.

Grant strode over, his expression serious. His face was tanned, and all sharp, jagged angles. He nodded to Jonas, then focused on her.

"Emily, since you're going ahead with your construction plans, I wanted to make sure you also take responsibility for all the wear and tear on our shared stretch of road. It's already taken a beating from those big trucks hauling in your lumber, and the cement mixers are going to eat it up. What you do to your driveway is your problem, but that section of common road—you'll have to fix any damages your crews cause. You understand?"

"Sure, Grant. If you see a problem, just let me know," she said, annoyed by his tone.

"There's an easy way for you to avoid all these problems, Emily. Let me buy you out. I'll exceed whatever property value estimates a Realtor comes up with by, say, ten percent?"

"Thanks, but as I told you the other day, I'm not interested in selling to you or anyone else. I intend to build my inn here. All the permits have been approved, and the work begins tomorrow."

"With all the setbacks you've been having, what makes you think anyone will want to patronize your motel?"

"Inn," she corrected. "And how do you know I've been having trouble?"

He gave her a wry smile, then turned and waved his arm. "I live just a mile and a quarter away. How could I miss the sirens and flashing lights running up and down the road? This used to be a quiet spot—until you came back home." He paused for effect, then added, "I liked it the way it was."

"Just give my business a chance. In the long run, you might like the changes it'll bring," she said.

"Doubtful, but it's your money." Grant started to go back to his truck, then stopped and reached inside his windbreaker. "I almost forgot. When I drove out to get my mail, I saw your box was full, so I picked it up, as well. You *do* know that the mailboxes are by the side of the highway now instead of at our gates? They changed that a couple of years ago."

"Sure. They're hard to miss. And thanks," she said, taking the bundle he handed her.

As he drove off, she removed the rubber band holding the

envelopes and catalogs together, and started to leaf through the stack. "He opened my bank statement!" she muttered, then shook her head. "No, never mind. I'm just thinking the worst because he annoyed me. It's possible it wasn't sealed properly."

Jonas took the envelope and studied it. "It's hard to tell one way or another, but that guy doesn't exactly make a great first impression. How long have you known him?"

"Since high school. Back then, he was a loner. The jocks would give him a hard time, shoving him around, and the girls avoided him because he creeped them out. He was overly nice— smarmy—and heaven help you if he had a thing for you."

"Did he? Have a thing for you, that is?"

"Me? No. I was a freshman when he was a senior, and just the girl next door who rode on the same school bus until he got his own car. The only time he ever paid any attention to me was when my mom disappeared." She saw Jonas nod absently, and realized that, like everyone else in the community, he'd heard the story.

After a moment, Emily continued, shifting the focus back to Grant. "But the older sister of a friend of mine ended up on Grant's radar, and things got bad in hurry. Right before spring break, he offered to give her a ride home. She took him up on it, but he drove her out into the *bosque* instead, then tried to make his moves. She ended up punching him where it hurts, then jumped out of his car and took off on foot."

"Did he get away with it otherwise?"

Emily shook her head. "Far from it. The girl's brother was on the wrestling team, and the next Monday morning Grant showed up at school with black eyes and bruises everywhere. After he got beat up a second time in a cafeteria fight, his parents put him in a private school for the rest of the year."

"Was there ever any problem with him stealing?" Jonas gestured to the stack of mail.

"Not that I heard. If anything, Grant was a victim—one of

those socially inept guys who went through school making more enemies than friends. He'd set himself up with his own inappropriate behavior."

Emily glanced at her father's workshop, then back at Jonas. "Before we get back to work, how about if I go get us something to drink from the fridge? Wet and cold."

"You've got beer?"

She made a face. "Yuck, no. What do you guys see in that stuff? But I can offer you a strawberry protein drink."

"Yeah, okay. As long as it's wet, I'm good."

It took her several minutes to mix the drink, then she placed the pitcher on a tray, with glasses, and headed back outside.

When she entered the workshop, Jonas stepped around the tall stack of boxes he'd made on a pallet. He'd stripped off his flannel shirt, and the ridges of hard muscle that covered his chest took her breath away.

She stared openly, unable to stop herself. His body had changed, matured in many ways. The scars on his chest spoke of battles fought—and won. He was far from the pretty-boy type who'd never met a mirror he didn't like. Yet there was something about Jonas that made her want to run her hands over him, taking a nip here and a taste there.

A knowing smile tugged at the edges of his mouth, and realizing she'd been staring—and maybe even drooling—she handed him his glass and stepped away.

"I've been rearranging the boxes to make more room," he said. He took a sip of the drink, scowled slightly, then took another.

As she looked past him into the far corner, now clear of items, something captured her attention. One of her father's favorite hiding places had been behind the old sawhorse that had stood there for years.

Stepping closer, she spotted a narrow gap between a gray electrical panel and the piece of thin wafer board that made up the unfinished interior wall. A piece of what looked like masking tape had come loose and was dangling down. The rest of the wall had been perfectly fitted, so it seemed out of place.

"There's something behind there," she said.

"There, where?" Jonas asked, following her gaze.

"Look just to the left of that circuit box or whatever it is. That narrow opening…"

He nodded. "I see it. All the other joints are perfect, yet that one spot has a shaved edge of wallboard."

"Let's peel back the tape and look inside," she suggested.

Reaching for the penlight in his pocket, Jonas aimed the beam into the small gap he'd uncovered. "There's something back there, all right, but it could just be more tape."

"Or not. Let's loosen the wallboard. This isn't a full-size four-by-eight piece, anyway. It's just a long strip."

Jonas went to the workbench and returned with a hammer and pry bar. "I've got it," he said, then carefully loosened the nails fastening the edge of the wood to the stud underneath. Once several were loose, he used the pry bar to pull the wallboard away a few inches, further loosening the nails.

As she watched his muscles rippling as he worked, desire coursed through her. Jonas was thrilling to watch, his body filled with raw power and strength. The temptation to touch him made her fingers tingle and sent flurries of longing all through her.

Realizing she was playing with fire and would no doubt be burned, she forced herself to look away.

"Help me pull this board off gently, so we won't break it," he said, turning to look at her.

"Yes, of course," she replied, her throat as dry as sand.

He flashed her a grin that spoke volumes.

Refusing to acknowledge it, she focused on the panel. "Okay, I'm ready," she said, grasping the bottom.

They wiggled the board back and forth, and after a minute or two, it came off, with a small cloud of dust.

The first thing they saw in the space they'd uncovered was a myriad of spiderwebs. One in particular merited their immediate attention. A large, shiny, black widow spider with an orange-red hourglass on her abdomen had spun her web across what appeared to be a rolled up piece of paper covered in plastic. The strong silk filaments of web held the spider in place, upside down, about six inches off the ground.

Jonas moved around Emily. "I hate to destroy the web, but she can make another. I'll scoop the spider into a shovel and take her outside."

"Just step on it, or squash it against the wall. Black widows are nasty, poisonous things."

He shook his head. "Spiders have their place. We're in no danger, and it's wrong to kill without a reason. Every action has a reaction, and the way to maintain the *hózhq,* the beauty and harmony in life, is to respect that everything serves a purpose. That's how a Navajo walks in beauty, by understanding the design and finding his place in it."

By the time Jonas returned from taking the spider outside, Emily had retrieved the paper and was brushing off what was left of the spiderweb.

"What've you got there?" he asked, peering over her shoulder as she slipped off the piece of string that had bound the paper.

"It looks like a sheet from a photo album or scrapbook." She studied the symbol drawn on the outside of the folded paper nested inside the plastic sleeve. Flames bounded by a circle… The image looked vaguely familiar. "I've seen this before somewhere. How about you?" she asked, showing it to him.

Although his face was now expressionless, she'd seen the flicker of recognition there. Maybe it was because her eyesight was fading and she was always pushing her visual limits, but she seldom missed nuances these days.

"I've seen it before, too. That's all I can tell you," he answered vaguely.

As she gazed back at the symbol, whispers of a memory echoed at the back of her mind, but she still couldn't place it.

"Let's see what your father went to so much trouble to conceal," Jonas pressed in a soft voice.

"I feel a little guilty opening it," she said with a sad smile, pulling the folded piece of paper out of the plastic. "But if it's part of the mess I inherited, I've got to know."

She wasn't sure what she'd expected, but the message inside answered no more questions than the rough penciled drawing on the outside. All it did was raise new ones. At the top of the sheet were the words *from Law Rock.* Below them were instructions to go in certain directions—measured in compass degrees, at set distances in yards or feet.

"The directions start from 'Law Rock' and obviously result in finding a specific location. But where's Law Rock?" Jonas murmured. He was all but certain there was no such geological formation in the area. "I'm familiar with most everything around here, but I've never heard of that particular formation."

"Me, neither," she answered, handing him the paper.

He stared at the directions, but at long last shook his head.

"This might be part of a game he set up for me—one we never actually got around to playing," she said slowly. "It's his style—and his handwriting. Like I told you, Dad loved games."

Jonas considered that. "Did your father have pet names for places around here, like a favorite spot along the cliffs or down by the river or on your property?"

"No. And for the record, I never heard him mention Law Rock."

"This could be what the men who broke into your father's office were after…or not. They did take old maps, right? Either way, without knowing where Law Rock is, the directions are all but useless." Jonas gazed at the symbol of the Brotherhood, the circle and the flames. "Or this might be a decoy. Something meant for others to find, a way to keep his enemy busy."

As Jonas moved away to make a call, Emily stared thoughtfully at the drawing of the circle and flames. It was so familiar, but she just couldn't place it, and the more she tried, the more elusive the memory became.

Chapter Four

Emily sat on the bench in the trailer. She'd studied the directions and distances so intently, looking for hidden meanings, she now had them memorized.

"My suggestion is that you keep it someplace safe," Jonas said. "It could be months before you figure out what that means."

He'd already checked with others in the Brotherhood. Within thirty miles, there was Ship Rock, Mitten Rock, Chimney Rock, Popping Rock, Thieving Rock and even Rock Ridge, but no one had ever heard of a place called Law Rock. They'd looked into the possibility that it was a translation, but had found nothing even close.

The brief talk he'd had on the phone with Diné Nééz continued to play in his mind. Grant Woods, as the resident closest to the accident scene, had been questioned as a potential witness. He had an alibi, apparently, which meant he couldn't have caused the car wreck that had killed Emily's father.

He'd been questioned a few hours ago about the other events, too. Grant claimed to have been at home, working in his office, during the first incident, and outside working on fence repairs during the second. He hadn't recalled hearing any vehicles, or a motorcycle.

"When Grant brought over my mail, it reminded me that I've yet to go through all the papers in Dad's safe-deposit box at the bank," Emily said, interrupting his thoughts. "Dad also had a post office box in town. That's where his business mail went because he didn't like leaving important papers in a rural mailbox."

"I don't blame him. There was a time around here when people didn't even lock their doors, particularly on the rez, but those days are long gone." Jonas stood. "Let me go change clothes, then we'll head into town. The reason I took off my shirt is because I ripped it against the corner of the workbench." He called her attention to the sleeve.

"Oh, I'm sorry. I thought you were hot." Her eyes grew wide and her face flushed crimson.

He laughed. "Well, I'm not exactly eye candy. I'm too scarred up."

"If you won those fights, I'd hate to see the other guy," she said with a smile.

He grew somber and shook his head. "I saw my share of action as a Ranger, but half the battles overseas are with an enemy you never see—as in mortar rounds and IEDs."

"I imagine things are very different for you now that you're working for the tribe."

Seeing the softness in her eyes as she gazed at him scrambled his brain, and for a moment he didn't answer. "Yeah, it's different," he said, cursing himself for getting distracted. "Give me a minute to change shirts. I've got clean clothes in my pickup. Then I'll be ready to go."

"I need to clean up, too. I'll meet you at your truck in a few minutes."

Emily changed into a clean pair of slacks and her favorite long-sleeved blouse. The ruffles around the collar had sold her on it. Though the garment was plain cotton, that small detail softened the look and gave it an extra feminine touch.

As she brushed her hair and tied it back into a ponytail, she focused on her future. The Tamarisk Inn would be a reality someday soon. It had taken her weeks to figure out what to call it. She'd finally decided to name it after the hardy plant that grew with its fragrant pink blossoms near the river *bosque.* It survived by finding just the right place for itself in the dry desert.

Moments later, she met Jonas by his pickup. He'd changed into a gray-blue shirt. The open collar revealed the very tip of the long, narrow scar she'd seen earlier. Scars meant experience, and the sight fueled her imagination. As far as she was concerned, Jonas was sexier than ever.

Pushing those thoughts back, Emily slipped into the passenger's side and fastened her seat belt. Everything in her life was upside down at the moment. Straightening things out—that's where her focus had to remain.

As they headed into town, she glanced around the cab of his truck. He had clothes on hangers, a backpack, a coil of rope and a locked metal box behind his seat. The rifle that hung on a rack over the rear window was almost standard equipment for rural New Mexico. The strange-looking radio with antennae was not.

"That looks like a police radio," she commented.

"I'm not a cop, but my work for the tribe requires top-notch communications equipment."

She had a million questions she wanted to ask him about his job as a vindicator, but knew he'd told her all he intended about that. "It looks like we both have our secrets," she said, and realized a moment too late that she'd spoken the thought out loud.

"Most of what I do has to remain confidential—to protect the clients."

"It's not just your job. You never talk about yourself—not at all."

"I'm boring. I'd rather know about you."

"Nice hedge." Emily smiled. "But if you want to earn someone's trust, you have to show that you trust them, too."

She could sense him trying to figure out how to respond, but after several long moments, she knew his silence was her answer.

As they continued the drive toward the city of Farmington,

her thoughts slowly shifted to other pressing concerns. "The tribe made my father an offer for a parcel of our land, the strip along the bluffs, and I haven't been able to find anything that suggests the deal was ever finalized. The county never recorded the transaction, either, according to conversations I've had on the phone. I also haven't had any word from the tribe, so I need to know if they're still interested. Who would you suggest I speak to?"

"I'm aware of the deal and I assure you the tribe is still interested. Would you like me to handle that for you?"

"Sure. I'd like to get that matter settled as soon as possible. That…was my father's last gift to me," she said, fighting the tears that tightened her throat.

Jonas reached out and took her hand in his. Even now, with sorrow bearing down on her, his touch soothed, and filled an empty spot inside her.

Emily took a deep breath and concentrated on the problems ahead. "The price for the land was already agreed to, so I'd like to finalize the paperwork and get payment as soon as possible. Truth is, I'll need the funds to complete the inn. The special amenities I need for my guests are very expensive, and my resources are stretched tight."

"Quick payment may not be possible," Jonas said after a momentary pause. "You wanted me to trust you, and I'm about to do that. But what I'm going to tell you has to remain between the two of us. Will you give me your word?"

"You have it," she said, excited by the fact that he was willing to confide in her.

"Our missing man was carrying the entire payment with him—in bearer bonds," he said. "Those have disappeared along with him."

"Does the tribe think he may have just run off with the money?"

"No. He's completely trustworthy. If he's running it's because someone's on his heels."

"Do you think my father's death is connected to the bonds?"

"It's possible, but there are other issues involved. The attack might be linked to some of the other work your father did for the tribe. But we don't know anything for sure yet."

"Except that I've become a target, and your man is missing, along with a great deal of money," she said.

Jonas nodded. "The threat to you is too well timed to be unrelated. If we can figure out who's coming after you, that should provide other answers, as well."

She sighed softly. "All I wanted was to build my inn—a place where I could always be useful and contribute to our community. It was a perfect idea, one meant to bring peace and good things. Yet all I've done is attract violence."

"No, that's not all," he said, brushing her face with his palm.

The tender gesture dissolved her defenses. Feelings and needs she'd sworn to ignore tore into her, tempting her, urging her to stop planning—stop thinking.

"You've got to fight for what you want," he added.

His words brought her back to reality. "And that's exactly what I intend to do."

He made it a point not to look at her. No one would have ever accused him of being weak willed, but all men had their vulnerabilities. Emily was his.

"We can't ignore what's going on between us," he said at last.

"No, we can't," she agreed, her voice a whisper. "But we don't have to give in to it, either. It can't lead anywhere…good."

"It *could* be good. Very good."

His voice was a deep rumble, and the vibrations coursed through her like fire, melting her insides. "For a while we'd find heaven. But afterward…"

"You'd regret it?"

Emily didn't answer. She couldn't. She was at war with herself, torn between logic and wanting to capture the wind—or just surrender and enjoy it while it lasted. But she needed more than stolen moments. The qualities she wanted in her future—roots, security—were the very things Jonas's nature urged him to avoid.

"I was sent to protect you," he said when she didn't answer. "And I'll see it done—even if it means protecting you from me."

He'd been "sent." He hadn't come of his own free will. Holding to that one fact, she drew into herself and said nothing more.

They were entering town, having turned off the truck bypass and onto Lake Street, when she felt the change in him.

"Slump down in the seat a little and keep your head away from the window," he murmured.

Alarmed, she instinctively did the opposite, sitting up and looking around anxiously. "What? What's wrong?"

"Get down," he insisted fiercely, his gaze on the rearview mirror. "Shortly after we left your property, a white pickup caught up to us, then passed us on the highway before we reached the bridge. Now it's back there once more, following us, though staying well back. When I slowed down to see what he would do, the driver turned west on the truck bypass. But he must have reversed course once he got out of sight, because he's behind us again."

"Do you want me to call the police?"

"No. As careful as he's been, my guess is that he'll disappear the second he knows we've made him. Let's play things a little differently."

As they entered the downtown area, Jonas turned right, on Main Street. Halfway down the block, he abruptly cut left into an alleyway between two multistory brick buildings.

"Get ready to jump out when I say so." They approached a small parking area set into a recess of the building. Next to it was a small loading dock.

"Just say when," Emily replied, feeling claustrophobic in the narrow urban canyon. She reached down, ready to press her seat-belt release.

Suddenly he slammed on the brakes. "Now!"

Emily jumped out, and by the time she reached the front of the truck, Jonas was already there, waiting. He grabbed her hand, pulling her toward the loading dock.

Once they were out of sight, he motioned with his head toward the corner. "Go back there and stay behind cover. I'll take care of this."

Before she could say anything, Jonas sprinted across the alley. With the pickup in the way, she lost sight of him almost immediately.

Emily kept her back to the brick wall of the former hotel, now an office building. A second later, she heard the sound of squealing tires, a shout, then a door opening.

Unable to suppress her curiosity, she peered around the corner. Jonas had ambushed the driver the moment he'd come to a stop, and yanked him out of the cab. Trying to get a clearer look, she turned her head, since the vision out of the corners of her eyes was better. With a gasp, she realized the other man was holding a gun.

Jonas gripped the driver's wrist and slammed it against the side of the cab. The blow knocked the gun free, and it flew into the bed of the pickup with a thud.

Jonas next delivered a powerful jab to the gut, doubling his opponent up. As he bounced off the open door, Jonas instantly pushed him down on the pavement, then wrapped his arms around the man's in a deadly hold.

Emily knew that with just one twist, Jonas could break his neck. That's when she saw the man's face.

"Jonas, stop!" she said, running out into the open. "That's Grant, my neighbor. Remember?"

Jonas hauled him to his feet, then shoved him over the hood of the pickup, his arm still at the man's throat. "I remember. What the hell are you up to, Woods?"

Jonas's voice was nothing more than a snarl, and it made her heart freeze. The gentle man she'd had beside her just seconds ago on the ride into town was gone, and in his place was someone she didn't recognize.

Chapter Five

"Talk fast, Woods," Jonas snapped, his gaze unyielding. "Why did you pull the gun?"

Grant made a choking sound but no words came out.

"He can't breathe!" Emily yelled, running over. Seeing the trickle of blood that ran from Jonas's knuckles onto the other man's shirt only accentuated her growing panic. "Let him go, Jonas!"

He eased his hold slightly. As he did, Grant choked again. "Back off!" he gasped at last. "You're hurting me."

"What did you expect me to do? You switched vehicles, followed us, then pulled a pistol."

"You jumped *me*. I was just trying to defend myself," he said, then began coughing.

"Talk—I'm not a patient man." Jonas pushed his forearm against Grant's throat again. "Why should I let you go? Give me a reason."

"Of course I was following. Don't you get it? When I passed you on the bridge, I realized Emily was with you. I hurried to catch up because I wanted to give her something. It's in my pocket."

Jonas moved back, releasing Emily's neighbor, but not taking his eyes off him.

Grant took two steps back, reached into his jacket, then brought out a legal-size envelope, which he handed to her.

"From our previous conversations I realized you probably weren't aware of this, Emily. When I offered to buy your land, that was in addition to the rights I already own."

"Rights? What are you talking about?" She opened the envelope and took out two pieces of paper.

"That's a copy of the contract between your father and me for drilling rights to the property—your land now. Although exploration costs are my responsibility, I'll now be splitting any royalties with you, since you're Powell's heir."

"This looks like Dad's stationery, and his signature, but he never said anything to me about this," she said, stunned by what she was holding. "I'm not sure if I'm bound by this agreement or not, Grant. I'll have to talk to my father's attorney and see what he has to say about it."

"You do that, but I think you'll find it's all perfectly legal."

"Until then, I don't want to say anything more," she announced in a hard voice.

"You heard the lady. Get lost, Woods," Jonas said.

Grant took another step back, then with one last look, walked over to the bed of his pickup.

"Leave the weapon there until you're out of our sight," Jonas warned.

He grumbled something, then climbed into his truck, threw it into Reverse and backed out of the alley.

Emily stared at the sheet of paper she held in her hands. "This is just crazy. I'm certain Dad would have told me about something like this."

"It bears checking out—closely. But in the meantime, try not to worry about it." Jonas started to put his arm around her shoulders, but she flinched.

Her reaction shook him to the core. "Now you're afraid of me?"

"No, it's just…" She paused, unable to continue.

His gaze locked with hers. "He pulled a gun, Em. That's as serious as it gets."

"I know," she said, trying to get her thoughts together, though her heart was still thundering in her ears. "*Nothing* makes sense to me anymore," she added, looking down at the paper and her shaking hands.

"You need a break from all this, and some fresh air will help, too. Let's go."

"Where?" she asked, following him to the truck.

"A place that never fails to put things back into perspective for me," he said as they climbed into the cab.

They drove southwest, out of the city. Instead of taking the first turn east past the river, they continued south, on a long, winding route that curved up onto the bluffs.

"Are we going far?" she asked.

"No, but you and I need to straighten some things out, and it's quiet up there." She'd been afraid of him and that cut deep. He had to fix this—and fast.

They soon reached the top of the big plateau, then drove east, parallel but south of her property. Jonas finally stopped and parked near the edge of the steep bluffs that overlooked the valley and city below. Like ancient stone warriors, sections of the cliff, broken loose below them and worn by erosion, stood in tall groups of three or more.

"Let's get out of the truck for a bit," he suggested.

They stood outside together for several long moments, listening to the wind that swept past them.

"I've hurt your feelings, haven't I?" Emily said at last.

"How could you be afraid of me?" he countered, meeting her eyes and holding them.

"Something ugly happened when you saw Grant's gun. I'd never seen that side of you," she said softly.

It felt as if she'd taken a knife and stabbed him in the heart. "My training is what will keep us both alive. It's not something you need to fear. And you should *never* be afraid of me."

"I know," she replied gently. "But for a few moments there, I was really afraid of what you might do to Grant." She took a long, deep breath. "I know that not too long ago you were a soldier fighting for your country, your buddies and your life. But you're home now, and this isn't a battlefield."

"Isn't it?" he growled.

"Not the same kind," she said softly.

"In a lot of ways it's exactly the same," he stated, turning away from her and looking off into the distance.

"In your heart you're still an Army Ranger, aren't you?' she observed slowly. "Why did you leave?"

"To answer that, I'd have to tell you why I joined, too."

She waited.

After a few minutes he spoke again. "I signed up for the Rangers because I wanted to get away from all the poverty and the sameness of life on the rez. Whenever I looked around, all I saw were people whose lives were marked only by the passage of time. I wanted to do something that really mattered. So I joined the toughest branch of the military I could find. I needed to prove that I had what it took to be the best."

He jammed his hands into his pockets. "Back in high school, our class went to D.C. on a field trip. In the House of Representatives chambers there's a quote carved into stone—'Something worthy to be remembered.' I wanted that to define what I'd become."

"As a Ranger did you find what you were looking for?"

"Partly, yes, but I also learned that everything comes at a price." He leaned back against one of the boulders and faced her. "Then, when I came home on leave after my last tour, I met a man from our tribe who convinced me that I was needed here. The time had come for me to serve my own people. That's why I stayed instead of reenlisting."

"Who was he, this man who changed your life?"

Shaking his head, Jonas smiled. "How do you do this? You

now know more about me now than just about anyone else on the planet."

"I'm worthy of your trust. Instinctively, you already know that, but your mind hasn't caught up yet," Emily said.

He laughed. "Is that your way of saying I'm all brawn and no brains?"

"No, of course not," she said quickly. Then, realizing he was just giving her a hard time, she added, "But after seeing your new bod shirtless, I've got to say that your brawn parts aren't bad at all."

He burst out laughing, then, acting on impulse, pulled her into his arms and lowered his mouth over hers. It was a soft kiss at first, but her mouth parted easily under his, and that was an invitation he couldn't resist. He tasted her, taking his time, losing himself in that moment of pleasure.

Hearing her sigh and feeling her melt against him heated his blood. His kiss suddenly turned hard and demanding. He devoured her mouth, taking all she would give, and still wanting more. Knowing that in another moment his control would be history, he finally eased his hold.

She looked up at him, her eyes unfocused, her chest heaving. It took everything he had in him not to pull her against him again.

"That…was…"

"A mistake?" he growled.

"I was going to say 'incredible.'"

As THEY HEADED BACK toward the city, she ran the tip of her tongue over her lips, still tasting him there. The way he'd held her, and all that passion barely kept in check… It had made her feel…powerful, to think she could do that to Jonas. Emotions clashed inside her and she realized that she had to get her mind on something else or she'd go crazy.

She gazed to the west. Ship Rock stood tall and alone, thirty miles away. She remembered her dad telling her once that the peak was sacred to the Navajo tribe. They believed it to be the remains of a huge bird that had once carried the Navajo People to safety.

"You never said who the man who changed your life was," she said.

"To many, he's known only as Dinétsoh."

She smiled. "I know him. He was a friend of my dad's." She remembered the first time she'd met him. Something about him had intrigued her right away. Beyond the playful eyes, she'd seen an intensity that had reminded her of the superheroes she'd been so fond of back then. Curious about him, she'd stopped by her father's office and listened outside the closed door.

Dinétsoh had told her dad that a very special group of individuals—the Brotherhood of Warriors—needed him to represent their interests. Dinétsoh had spoken of the group as "the men of the circle and the flames." He'd said that they were the tribe's best warriors—ones who operated in the shadows so others could walk in beauty.

As she looked at Jonas, Emily suddenly knew with absolute certainty who and what he was. The cryptic message her father had hidden in his workshop was somehow connected to the Brotherhood, too.

Jonas's eyes narrowed. "What? You have a very peculiar expression on your face."

"Nothing," she said. What Dinétsoh had told her father had been a tribal secret. Once she'd heard that, she'd instantly felt guilty. As a way of making up for what she'd done, she'd kept the secret, as well—her way of honoring both men. "I was just thinking about the nature of secrets...."

Jonas studied her expression before focusing back on the road. "Sometimes keeping them is a matter of honor. At other times it's just a way to insure you can face a battle on your own terms."

His words caught her attention. She knew his secret. Had he guessed hers? Had he seen her looking askance at something at one time or another when she was trying to see it more clearly? What was happening to her sight was something she'd wanted to keep private, at least for now. The possibility that he already knew made her feel vulnerable and exposed.

"We each have things we don't speak about, but there's nothing wrong with that," he continued. "Anglos usually talk too much. They want everything out in the open, but that's not always the best way. Navajos believe that to speak of something is to risk making it come true. That's why we're more careful about what we say."

"I can respect that, but I miss the days when trust came more easily," she said wistfully, remembering her teens.

"Trust is earned, not by what's said or isn't, but by actions. Judge me on that basis, and I'll do the same for you."

"You've got yourself a deal," Emily answered with a smile. She knew what she needed to know about him. He'd fight—for her and his tribe—and never quit till the job was done. That was enough. As long as she kept a firm rein on her heart, she'd be fine.

AFTER FINDING NOTHING but junk mail at the post office, they went to the bank to check out her father's safe-deposit box. Maybe some of the answers she needed would be stashed away there. After that, she'd speak to her father's real-estate attorney and find out more about the contract Grant Woods had presented to her.

Since she'd already been to the box once since her father's death, all the legalities had been settled. With her right to access the box assured, and key in hand, she wrote her name on the sign-in sheet and followed the attendant to the vault.

Carrying the big metal inner drawer for her, Jonas went with her into one of the small cubicles set aside for privacy. Emily sat in the chair before the desk, while he remained standing to her right.

Although it was difficult for her to read in subdued light, she skimmed through the papers as best she could, setting aside those that seemed important.

"It appears Dad kept all the written offers he ever got for our property. This first one goes back twenty years. It's from a gas company that wanted the drilling and mineral rights."

She studied the next sheet, angling it to get the best lighting. "Here's a land offer from Grant Woods. It dates back three years, right after his mother died, if I remember correctly. His father had already passed on, so he inherited everything."

Emily read the offer again, more carefully this time. "But this isn't for drilling rights—this is for the entire ranch. The note at the bottom, written in my dad's hand, shows the date he rejected the offer."

"Interesting," Jonas murmured, looking down at the contract.

"My dad wouldn't have signed over drilling rights to Grant and not kept a copy of the agreement. He was very detail oriented. As you can see, he kept a copy of everything."

"Let me have some of my contacts look over the document Woods handed you. It might be a forgery, but it's a very clear copy, so it should give them enough to work with. We have samples of your father's signature on record and can have expert comparisons made. Is that okay with you?"

"Sure. You'll let me know as soon as possible what your people find out?"

"Of course." He eyed the rest of the papers from the drawer. "No maps, so their loss still remains a mystery. Did you see anything in there that mentions or explains what Law Rock is?"

"I didn't, but feel free to take a look." She reached for the unlabeled envelope she'd set aside, and pulled out the single sheet of paper it contained. "Here's something with that tribal emblem—the circle and the flames. But it's not an offer. It's a contract between the Tribal Special Interests Authority and Dad, stating that he's their legal representative and will look after their interests." She smiled. "Hey, and it's signed by Dinétsoh!"

Jonas had meant to ask how she knew that the circle and the flames were tribal in origin, but something in her voice when she mentioned Dinétsoh diverted him. "How well did you know him?"

She smiled. "I was only a kid when I first met him, but he was always nice to me. He'd come to the house often to talk to Dad about business, and whenever he did, he'd take time for me, too. We went hiking once or twice. He even taught me how to track."

"When's the last time you saw him?" Jonas asked quickly.

There was an edge to his voice that told her it wasn't an idle question, and that her answer was important. She considered for a moment before answering. "It's been years…probably just before I moved away to college. Once I left home, I seldom came back to visit."

She bumped into the drawer with her elbow, and as she turned around, something caught her eye. "There's a scrap of paper stuck to the inside of the drawer, near the hinge," she said, leaning in for a closer look. "It's taped to the top."

"Be careful. Don't tear it," he said.

After removing the folded sheet, a piece of her father's stationery, she unfolded it on the desktop. "It's another puzzle," she said. "This time it's a collection of numbers and the letters *n, e, w, d, m* and *s*. Do they make sense to you?" she asked, handing Jonas the sheet.

He studied the information, then glanced back up at her. "They look like map coordinates—latitudes and longitudes of different locations in the same vicinity. They're the same degrees and minutes. Only the seconds are different."

"Could these be the coordinates to the place he mentioned before—Law Rock?"

"The coordinates aren't specific enough to give us an *exact* location—not unless Law Rock is the size of a house. And there wouldn't be three of them."

The muted light in the cubicle was a constant annoyance to

her as she struggled to read. It was also a reminder of the fight she was losing. "I'll put the contract offers back where I found them, but I'm keeping the coordinates with me."

"Would you like me to check them out and see if any correspond to locations on your property? All it'll take is one phone call."

"Yeah, go ahead," she said without hesitation.

Emily watched him leave the vault area, then, alone, placed everything back. By the time she'd finished, he still hadn't returned, so she went outside to where they'd parked.

She found him on his cell phone, speaking in Navajo. Seeing her, Jonas finished up quickly. "I'm having someone run those coordinates right away."

"Someone you trust, I hope?"

"With my life," he said. "One of the advantages of my work for the tribe is that it gives me access to people with special skills."

"Let's hope we get answers soon." Emily glanced up at the street sign and added, "Robert Jefferson's office is around the corner. He's my father's attorney. Let's drop by there and see if he's available. I'd like his opinion on the contract Grant handed me. I'm hoping he'll say it isn't binding. That would solve all the problems."

"If it does turn out to be legitimate, the tribe will probably want to redraft the terms of the sale," he warned. "We won't grant drilling rights—not easily, anyway."

Her stomach plummeted. With those few words he'd given voice to one of her worst nightmares. Without the money from the sale, she wouldn't be able to furnish the inn, or hire the necessary staff, much less build her own casita.

Knowing that the odds were stacked against her, Emily reached deep within herself for the courage she needed. Some dreams were worth fighting for. "Let's see what Robert has to say, then I'll decide what needs to be done next."

THEY ARRIVED AT THE attorney's small but elegant ground-floor office a few minutes later. A young, curvy, dark-haired woman sat at the front desk. She answered a telephone call, then glanced up at them. "Hello. Ms. Atkins, isn't it? I'm Jen Caldwell. How can I help you today?"

"I'd like a few minutes with Robert if he's available, Jen. I need to discuss a real-estate matter."

The woman looked down at a desk calendar for a second, then glanced back to Emily. "He's clear for the next hour. If this concerns the Grant Woods offer, I don't think Mr. Jefferson has the paperwork finalized yet."

"Are you talking about a property offer, or something to do with the mineral and drilling rights?" Emily asked.

"Property, unless Robert—Mr. Jefferson—has had further contact with Mr. Woods since his last visit." Jen hesitated a moment, then added in a low voice, "I know this isn't any of my business, but I hope you reject Mr. Woods's offer and sell to someone else. There's something really creepy about that man."

"What happened? Did he start hanging around, and now you just can't seem to get rid of him?" Emily asked.

"How'd you know?"

"Back in high school he had a thing for petite, dark-haired girls with your type of figure. He fawned over them, which tended to drive them nuts after a while."

Before Emily could continue, a tall, portly man appeared from the adjoining office.

"Emily, how are you doing?" he said, shaking her hand. "Again, I'm so very sorry about your father."

She nodded but said nothing. People meant well, but every reminder of her loss opened a wound that hadn't healed yet.

"Come into my office," Robert said, then glancing at Jen, added, "Hold my calls."

Emily introduced Jonas as a family friend, and Jefferson invited them to take a seat. Walking to a coffeemaker on a large credenza, he added, "I have a special brew made from piñon nuts—produced by a New Mexico company, naturally. Would you like some? But I warn you, I make it strong."

She shook her head. "No, thanks."

When Jonas also declined, Robert walked to his desk, sat in the extra large leather chair and leaned back. "So, tell me, Emily, what I can do for you today?"

She handed him the contract Grant had given her. "This is a copy of a deal Grant claims to have made with my dad just before he died. My father never mentioned this to me, and I haven't been able to find the original document anywhere among Dad's papers. Do you remember drawing up this contract?"

Jefferson studied the paper for a moment. "I was your father's attorney, but this isn't my work. That doesn't mean it's not genuine—it could have been handled by another attorney or even a Realtor—but I have to say it surprises me. Your father always checked with me when it came to real-estate matters. He was a thorough person. You know that."

"Yes, he was," she stated.

The lawyer continued to study the contract for several more moments, then looked up at her. "There's something else I find confusing about this contract. Just recently Mr. Woods made it clear to me that he intends to expand his land holdings while the market is depressed, then sell off parcels once the prices go back up. So why go the direction of gas exploration? As far as I know, he has no contacts or experience in that industry."

"Is it binding on me?" Emily asked.

"You said you couldn't find the original?"

"No, and I've gone through everything," she said.

"The first thing you need to do is make sure it's a legitimate contract. There's a county records number at the top, so apparently the papers were filed. That would be the next place to check. If it's all legal, you may have to take him to court to get it thrown out. That could get dicey, but I'll give it a try for you, if you want."

"Thanks, Robert. Give me a few days to follow up on this, then I'll get back to you."

"No problem," he answered. "Are you still going forward with your plans to build the inn?"

"To the extent I can, yes, but my funds are low and I've had someone sabotaging me every step of the way," she said, explaining about the vandalism and the break-ins.

"Be careful, Emily. A lot of people would like to get their hands on your property. That's prime real estate," he said. "I haven't done all the credit checks on Grant yet, but so far, it appears he has the financial resources to pay top dollar. But this rights agreement does sound a bit odd. Maybe he has a backup strategy ready in case he has to buy you out one step at a time."

"Thanks for your help, Robert," she said, standing to shake his hand.

Moments later, Jonas and she were outside. "Back to the ranch?" he asked.

"Yeah, I'd like to check up on the work done today," she replied. "I'd always intended on being very involved with the day-to-day activity. But nothing's gone the way I planned."

"Maybe you'll be able to get back on track by the time the foundation is laid and the actual framing begins."

She didn't answer, her heart heavy. Judging from the way things were going, she saw no reason to believe the situation would improve anytime soon.

Yet as she glanced at Jonas, she found reason to hope. Life was about the unexpected and no one could predict the future. The fact that Jonas was here now was ample proof that fate had its own plans for her.

Chapter Six

As they headed back to the ranch, Emily replayed Robert Jefferson's words in her mind.

"I keep thinking that I'm missing something important, Jonas, but I have no idea what that could be."

"Too many questions are coming at you at once, Em. Don't let it bug you. The answers are there, and we'll find them."

There had been no deviation in his tone, no uncertainty. "You're always so sure of yourself. Is it just confidence?"

He gave her a devastatingly masculine grin. "Some, sure. But a lot of it is experience at this job."

"You left the rez for some very specific reasons, and poverty—for one—is still there. What makes you more able to accept that now?"

"Dinétsoh and I were talking one day and I told him I couldn't understand how anyone could be happy living hand-to-mouth, subsistence farming in the desert, and herding sheep. He told me that I was looking at things wrong, and took me with him to an isolated area of the rez. There, he introduced me to some of the people I'd categorized as having nothing except desperation and poverty."

"And that changed your mind?" she asked, surprised.

He nodded slowly. "There was more to their lives than I'd realized. Our eyes fool us into thinking that the picture before us is the whole story, but that's not always so, and it certainly wasn't in this case. The goal of a good Navajo isn't acquisition of goods, or even personal comfort. It's to walk in beauty. To understand why they'd chosen that life, I had to reacquaint myself with the Navajo Way."

"You mean, Navajo religion?"

"Something like that. The closest word we have for *religion* is *nahaghá,* which means that a ceremony's under way," he said. "Our people are guided by certain traditions. Those teach us how to live our lives. That's the Navajo Way. The Diné believe that we're all connected—animals, people, the land. Knowing that, and respecting the connection that binds us all together, is what allows a Navajo to find balance and harmony, and that's how we walk in beauty."

"Sounds like a good way to live," she said.

"It is, and reconnecting to it was the right thing for me. So I had an Enemy Way done, remained home and began to work for the tribe."

"An Enemy Way?"

"It's a ceremony that allows a returning soldier to restore harmony within himself. Once that was done, everything else fell into place."

So much about Jonas drew her, but she knew that he was a free spirit who needed the freedom his lifestyle gave him. Accepting what she couldn't change, she tore her thoughts away from him and looked at the path ahead.

They were just making the turn onto the highway that ran parallel to the bluffs, and led to her home, when his phone rang. Jonas pulled over to the shoulder and stopped to answer. He spoke softly in Navajo, then ended the call. "The coordinates have been checked, and they match points on your land."

"Did your contact have any idea why my father targeted those particular locations?"

"All we've been able to determine is that there are old coal mine shafts in that general area."

She nodded. "The mines date back to the eighteen hundreds, I've been told. Maybe Dad flagged those shafts so he'd know exactly where they were. Let's go take a look around." Her own choice of words made her pause and think. The day would come when she'd have to learn another way of getting around in a sighted world.

"Why don't I go track down those places on my own? I've noticed that your eyes are giving you problems from time to time. If those shafts run along the cliffs, you're going to need to be very sure-footed."

Emily's first instinct was to deny that she had a problem, but then decided against it. "It's true that my eyesight's bad in low light, but I'm just fine when the sun's up," she answered.

"If you don't mind my asking, what exactly is the problem with your vision?"

She didn't answer right away, taking time to gather her thoughts. "You told me recently that Navajos are careful about what they say out loud. It's like that for me, too, though my reasons are different. I don't talk about my eyesight because people tend to sympathize and pity too easily. Or, if they care, they'll try to overprotect, and eventually smother. I can't allow myself to accept any of that, because it's a sure road to defeat."

Jonas nodded slowly. "I agree with you about that, but I also know that you're not the kind who can accept defeat, not without one heck of a fight."

His belief in her bolstered her confidence and strengthened her. "Thank you for saying that."

"It's the truth."

"Now you also understand why I have to take an active role in finding answers, and can't just hand things over to you or anyone else. Some of it is pride, yes," she admitted, "but there's more to it than that. My future's at stake, and it's my responsibility to see things through."

"Just don't try to shoulder everything by yourself. No one ever stands alone."

"Is that part of the Navajo belief? That we're all connected?"

Jonas nodded, then gave her a devilish grin. "And some of us are more connected than others."

To her credit, Emily didn't choke, but his deep voice and the memory he'd evoked jolted her to the core.

"Do you ever think of that night?" she asked after several long moments, her voice almost a whisper.

"More than you realize. That memory saw me through some very bad times," he said. "I can still see you stumbling around in the blizzard, hypothermia about to set in, your jacket and pants sopping wet. You couldn't stop shivering by the time we made it to my shelter. I got you out of those wet clothes, then crawled into the sleeping bag with you. I knew my own body heat was needed to keep you alive." Then, in a smoldering voice that came from the depths of him, he added, "The rest…what happened hours later…was nature and fate."

"I remember every detail of that weekend," Emily whispered. His body against hers… At first she'd felt nothing but numbness. Then cold, then heat—the blazing kind that was all consuming. He'd been the first and only man she'd ever made love to. After that night, no one else had mattered.

He brushed his knuckles against the side of her face, then forced his eyes back on the road. "We're both different people now, Em. So much has happened to us since that night."

"Your work…it's everything to you."

He could have argued the point, but there was too much truth in what she'd said. "Yes. I'm good at what I do, and my work's needed."

"And you're the best among the best," she murmured, thinking of the Brotherhood.

Her words caught his attention. Yet as he studied her expression, he could read nothing on her face. "So where to next?" he asked, weaving more than one meaning into his words.

"Drop me off at my trailer. I need to put on a pair of hiking boots, then we'll set out."

"Boots are a good idea. This time of day rocks provide shelter for snakes, and there's no telling when you'll run into one."

As they drove through her open gate, they saw three workmen's trucks parked nearby. The sound of hammers and pry bars came from inside the main house. Today, built-ins and woodwork she wanted to keep, such as the big stone pass-through, were being removed. They'd be stored, and then at the right time brought back to be used in the new structures.

Ken, the tall, slender construction foreman, stepped out onto the porch as they drove by, and gave them a thumbs-up.

Jonas took Emily directly to the trailer, and five minutes later, they set out on foot, wearing small day packs containing water, flashlights, gloves, binoculars and climbing rope.

He was armed with his pistol, not for snakes, but for protection against possible intruders. After the previous two incidents, it didn't made sense to take chances. The next attack, if there was one, might involve something lethal—knives or firearms.

They decided to hike to the closest location first—southeast, and close to Woods's property line.

Emily matched Jonas's pace. It had been years since she'd hiked this far from the house. Her parents had left the natural vegetation intact, so they were quickly within the upper limits of the *bosque*—the cottonwood forest that lined the river bottom and upper banks.

On most of the other properties along the populated valley, the *bosque* had been cleared for fallow and cultivated fields. Here on her land there were thickets of tamarisk, Russian olives and willows, and, closer to the river, flats of salt grass, sandbars and dunes.

Emily knew this valley well, as did most New Mexicans who lived in rural farming communities. It was no accident that the city just to the north had been named Farmington.

The land sloped gently uphill, becoming drier and rockier as they approached the towering bluffs. Here, sagebrush and grama grass were more common, and a few low, fragrant junipers dotted the land.

They'd been hiking for close to thirty minutes, and the side of the valley was getting steeper, when she stopped, needing time to catch her breath. "How much farther?" she asked, looking back toward the house, but not able to see it anymore because of the trees.

"Maybe another ten minutes, according to the GPS reading," he said, reaching into his backpack and taking out a bottle of water. Although he'd made it a point to search for any signs of Dinétsoh as they'd covered ground, he'd yet to find any indication that the man had come this way.

"It's a nice day for this kind of hike, with the weather in the sixties."

Before he could reply, they both heard a rustling in the brush to their right. Jonas reached for the pistol, tucked into a holster at his belt, hidden beneath his jacket.

A second later a coyote appeared in full view. The animal stopped, watched them for a second, then trotted quickly to the north, keeping his distance as he headed toward the river. Ducks and other waterfowl had been returning from their winter migration for a few weeks now, and the food supply for hunters and scavengers was on the increase.

"I know that to a lot of people, coyotes are just a nuisance, but I've always liked having them around," Emily said. "Of course, I imagine it's totally different for a sheep herder. Do Navajos hate them?"

"No, not 'hate.' That's too strong a word. Coyote has his place. In our creation stories, the gods who stood for good always stayed on the south side of all the gatherings. The evil ones took their place on the north. Coyote, being neither good nor evil; took his post near the doorway. That way he could choose either side, depending on his mood. Many call him the Trickster. It's his unreliability that made warriors turn and head in the opposite direction whenever they saw a coyote on the trail."

"And now that we have, would you like to take a detour? We could go the long way around."

"He didn't really cross our path," he said with a trace of a smile.

As they looked back downhill in the direction the animal had gone, something whined overhead. Almost simultaneously, the crack of a gunshot came from behind them.

Jonas pushed her to the ground beside a low, wide bush, then urged her over another two feet, behind the protection of a sandstone boulder. After looking her over quickly to make sure she was okay, he gestured for her to remain where she was.

Jonas slipped off his backpack, then crawled away, low to the ground, dragging the pack along by the strap.

Memories of other battles filled his mind, but with effort, he focused solely on the present. The shot had come from roughly the same direction where the coyote had been. Maybe a hunter had been on its trail.

Nearly invisible now behind some thick brush, he reached into the backpack and removed the binoculars. Before he could focus the lenses, he heard someone approaching.

The shooter was noisy, making little effort to hide his presence. Jonas drew out his pistol, thumbing off the safety.

Soon an Anglo man carrying a rifle at quarter arms appeared from behind a juniper, then stepped right into Jonas's field of fire.

Gun in hand, Jonas rose to a crouch, and verifying with his peripheral vision that no one else was coming along behind the shooter, stood. "Stop, and don't make another move. If you swing that rifle around, I'll drop you."

The man froze, his head turning as he spotted Jonas. "I

didn't know anyone else was around. I was after that darned coyote. It must have passed by close to here. Didn't you see it?"

Jonas took the rifle away from the man, removing the clip and ejecting a .22 Long Rifle round from the chamber. "Who are you?"

"Who are *you?* Some kind of *bosque* cop?"

"I'm the one with the pistol. Answer the question."

"Sam Carpenter's the name. I'm Grant Woods's handyman," he said. "I'm fixing up an old cabin of his just below the bluffs about two miles over." He turned to point.

"I said don't move," Jonas growled, laying the rifle across the top of a bush, then placing his pistol back in the holster.

"Relax!" the man answered.

Emily came out from behind cover then and walked up to them. "The Woods property line is at least five hundred yards east of here. What are you doing, hunting on *my* land?"

"Your land? You're Emily Atkins." He shrugged helplessly. "Sorry, there aren't any fences this close to the bluffs, and I was after that coyote. I must have lost track of where I was."

"Nobody hunts *any* creature on *my* land," she repeated.

"And shooting without a clear target can get somebody killed," Jonas snapped. "Your bullet flew right over us."

"I never even saw you or the lady. I wasn't expecting anyone to be out here." He glanced down at the rifle. "I'm going to need the .22 back. It belongs to Grant—Mr. Woods."

Jonas handed him the clip. "Don't load it again until you're off Atkins property. And if any other bullets come our way, accidental or not, I'm going to come hunting for *you,*" he said, his voice dropping an octave and vibrating with a lethal edge.

"Yeah, okay," Carpenter mumbled, reaching down and gingerly picking up the rifle. He backed away a few steps, then turned and moved east at a fast pace.

"The shot he fired…it really came close to us, didn't it?"

Emily looked down at the cartridge Jonas had ejected from the rifle, picked it up and handed it to him.

He looked at the round, then put it in his pocket. "Carpenter's either an excellent shot or a miserable one. If he really was trying to hit the coyote, he was firing blind, and aiming at movement—which turned out to be ours. But if what he really intended was to shake us up with a near miss, he was right on the mark."

"I never want to hear a bullet whistle overhead like that again," she said with a shudder.

"Would you like to turn back?"

"No." She sighed. "We've come too far to waste all that time and effort. He's gone, so let's complete what we started," she said, her voice stronger now.

"All right. But let's stick close to cover, and avoid long, open stretches from now on."

"You know, maybe there's something to the stories about Coyote," Emily commented, coming up beside him.

Jonas didn't answer. His gaze remained focused on the land around them. "If you hear anything strange, be ready to react in a hurry."

After another five minutes he checked his GPS and confirmed that they were close to the spot. He knew that this particular area had been searched with thermal imagining. Brotherhood warriors had also followed up with a ground search for Dinétsoh. He could see fresh prints here and there, probably left by his brother warriors who, when tracking, wore untraceable footware.

Jonas remained alert for subtler signs. Dinétsoh was said to have been wearing ordinary street shoes at the time. Yet, despite that, any trail left by his mentor would be defined by infinitesimally small clues—ones most others would overlook.

As they hiked, he kept an eye out for things such as a man-made scratch on a boulder, or one rock stacked on another. Even two sticks crossed. But all he found was the distinctive trail of a cottontail—long hind legs and short front paws.

As they came into a rocky passageway, something immediately caught his eye.

Emily came up behind him almost at the same time. "It's broken—snapped in half—at eye level," she said, pointing to a juniper branch. "That brings back memories."

"Of what?"

"When I was a kid, Dinétsoh taught me about tracking, and how to leave trails someone else could follow in case I ever got lost. A branch broken at eye level like that was one of his favorite techniques."

Chapter Seven

It took Jonas a beat to gather his wits. "That's a good call. A marker like that is meant for someone who's watching for a sign. It's the kind of thing that's easy to overlook or dismiss."

Jonas studied the branch. The break was relatively fresh—at least fresh enough to fit the important time frame. He was sure now that Dinétsoh had come this way and, more important, had wanted someone to know about it.

"Do you think this was left by the Navajo man who was with my father? I mean, why resort to leaving a trail like this unless you don't have any other option?" She looked at the ground. "At least Carpenter didn't come this way. I noticed that he left very distinctive work-boot prints."

Jonas was thinking of Dinétsoh, wounded, on the run from an assailant and trying to find his way to safety. There wasn't enough ground cover here to hide anyone in daylight—not for long—and certainly not from an overhead thermal search at night. So the question of where he'd gone remained. Above, on the bluffs but still almost a quarter mile away, were the old mines. Some had undoubtedly collapsed after decades of weathering and erosion. If that was the shelter he'd chosen, only more danger awaited him there.

"Be careful stepping on or around the rocks that have tumbled down from the heights. You could break an ankle—or worse," he said as they continued on.

"You're also thinking about rattlesnakes," she said quietly, fully aware of the danger. "Don't worry. I've done lots of hiking."

After they'd walked another fifty feet, Emily stopped. "You just reminded me of something. One time when I was playing with Dinétsoh, he left a fetish by a rock for me as a clue that he'd been there. I remember him specifically saying that it was a clue most would miss, since the rocks posed their own danger."

Jonas nodded slowly. Although she didn't know that Dinétsoh was the missing man, Emily's tracking skills were worthy of the teacher who'd taught them to her.

"It would be better if you look around while I keep an eye on the general area," he said.

The bluffs were still too far away to offer any threat except from a high-powered rifle in the hands of an expert sniper. He and Emily were also high enough up the valley to have a good view of the terrain to the north. The east and western flanks offered cover, but he wasn't going to be taken off guard again.

"I've got something," she called out. "Look in the recess of that large rock just off the little trail. The fetish is in partial shadow right now, but in the morning hours it would show up as clear as anything."

Jonas stepped past her and retrieved the small wood carving. "It's an ant fetish. Ants are all about patience," he said, remembering. "They can be aggressive when need be, and are known for having the energy to complete whatever task is before them."

"That was Dinétsoh's spiritual brother," she said with surprise.

"Don't jump to conclusions," he cautioned, wondering how long he'd be able to keep the truth from her. "There are many others who carry fetishes, and Ant isn't uncommon. It could have been left by a hiker. There are outdoor clubs who leave messages and artifacts for others to uncover."

"Letterboxing," she said with a nod. "It's getting popular

now. People combine hiking with sleuthing as they try to find messages others left behind. But I doubt this is something like that. Maybe your missing man…" She didn't complete the thought, hoping he'd fill in the rest.

Jonas didn't want to answer her, so he kept silent. He couldn't be sure of anything at this point, but he was more determined than ever to stay on the trail.

They'd gone less than fifty yards more when she spotted an arrowhead on the ground. She bent down to retrieve it, then suddenly stopped.

"I collect arrowheads," Emily explained. "They're really hard to find. Would it bother you if I took it?" she asked, remembering what he'd said about the *chindi*.

"I'd rather you leave it where it is. Those belong to the Old Ones, the `Anaasází. Leaving their belongings intact and undisturbed shows respect for who they were."

"All right."

"The coordinates we've been looking for are very close now, maybe fifty feet," he said, checking the display on the GPS.

They went a little farther, and found gray potshards and rocks arranged in a circle at what might have been a fire pit— or maybe part of an `Anaasází shelter. "An old encampment— or it might have been a dwelling," he said.

"This must be why Dad marked this location." Emily said nothing else for several long moments, then finally asked the question foremost in her mind. "Is Dinétsoh the missing man you've been searching for?"

Jonas said nothing.

"Don't you think I've earned the right to know?"

"I work for the tribe. As it was for your father and his clients, there are certain confidences that have to remain privileged."

"Dinétsoh was my friend, too," she said softly.

There was nothing else he could say. He'd tell Diné Nééz as

soon as possible, and hope he'd be allowed to at least confirm what she already knew in her heart.

"Maybe the Law rock is around here," she said, looking for a mark on a rock, or maybe rocks arranged in an L. After a fruitless five-minute search, they moved on.

They soon reached another open area where the placement of crudely shaped rocks suggested three structures had once stood there. They also found many more pottery shards—white pieces with black painted designs, black designs on red ceramic, and some with a corrugated pattern that looked like a stylized weave.

"I have a feeling this is a big part of the reason Dad was concerned about these parcels. There are no signs of digging anywhere, so pot hunters and vandals don't yet know this is here."

"Let's take another look around for that L rock," Jonas said.

They circled the site, found nothing, then moved in the general direction of the next coordinate. All traces of the `Anaasází site soon disappeared, giving way to an open area of tall grasses punctuated by an occasional juniper.

Jonas stopped, checked the GPS, then looked for any low ground or arroyos they could use to cross the clearing without making themselves easy targets. Although no one would be able to hide in ambush in their immediate vicinity, the two of them would be sitting ducks for a gunman positioned among the tumbled rocks at the base of the bluffs, or higher.

"Let's circle this open area, staying just within the trees, and stick to cover whenever possible."

He led the way. Fragments of the large stones and rubble that had fallen, victims of wind, water and gravity, provided good cover.

"Stop," he said suddenly. Apparently someone or something else had made the same decision—to seek cover. Yet the amount of dried blood that stained the flat surface of the sandstone trail worried him.

"That blood…it's from an injured animal, right?" Emily asked, her tone betraying the sudden fear that gripped her.

"There's no way to know for sure. But this much blood and no body means that whatever it was must have been big enough to take a hit. Maybe Sam Carpenter has been hunting this area, as well, and put a bullet in a wild dog, coyote or even a lost calf. He acted a little trigger happy."

"Could it have been a mountain lion…or a man?" she asked in a strangled voice.

He nodded and continued studying the pattern of blood on the ground. The shape and distribution suggested the victim had stopped here for a while, maybe trying to find a way to stem the flow. There was no discernible trail leading away in any direction, and that fact suggested the intelligence of an experienced tracker.

Jonas was glad to note that Emily had moved closer to him. He was constantly aware of her, and seeing her instinctively turn to him for safety satisfied everything male in him.

Angry with himself for getting distracted, he muttered a curse. He needed to focus on the danger, not the proximity of a beautiful woman.

His gaze took in the immediate area. Something didn't feel right. Trusting his instincts, he took point and led the way up through the rocks, his gaze on the ground before them.

"What's that?" she asked, gesturing beyond a gap in the tree line.

Taking a few steps back to place himself in Emily's sight line, he followed her gaze and saw a woman's leather tote bag hanging from a juniper branch at eye level.

Emily stepped toward it, but he quickly grabbed her shoulder.

"Impulse moves lead to trouble. Wait until I check this out."

"A woman hiker probably lost it. Maybe the ruins have been attracting more passersby than I thought." She paused. "Wait a minute. Most hikers don't carry handbags."

"Exactly. They use backpacks," he answered. "Things that practically scream for attention always send up a red flag for me. Overseas, the enemy would booby trap innocent-looking objects people were likely to pick up or examine."

He bent over, picked up a long stick, then moved it gently across the surface of the ground ahead of his feet. After several steps, he stopped. "There's a thin wire right here," he said, pointing Navajo-style by pursing his lips.

He crouched and, moving his hand along the barely visible line, lifted leaves away with his fingertips. A small canister device about the size of a shotgun shell was mounted on a stake driven into the ground. It was angled upward in line with the dangling purse, the clear line attached to the bag and the device.

"Step back and to the left," he said quickly.

"What's that, a firecracker?"

"It's an M44, something government hunters and ranchers have been known to deploy. It's used mostly to kill coyotes. The animal pulls on the bait at the top and a spring inside it shoots a sodium cyanide capsule into the animal's mouth. But this has a line attached, and pulling on the purse sets it off."

"The purse is the bait, and since this is my land, *I'm* the target?" she said, her voice rising.

"The chances of you or anyone other human being actually hurt by this kind of trap, one that requires you to take the pellet into your mouth, is slim to none. That means it was meant to be found and used only to scare you—or set you up for something else." Jonas studied the ground, noting where it had been smoothed out, probably with a leafy branch, to get rid of any distinguishing shoe prints. "We're not in the clear yet. Can you see your previous footprints?"

"I think so," she said, looking back.

"If you're not absolutely sure, then stay put. Once I deactivate this trap, I'll probe around for another. Traps meant for people are often set in pairs—one for the wary victim to find, and the other to do damage," he said, choosing his words carefully.

Jonas had seen cyanide traps when he was back in high school on the rez. Bubonic plague, rabies, hantavirus and other issues were common in the Four Corners, and those often resulted in aggressive animal-control measures. He'd also had plenty of field experience with bombs, IEDs and a host of other booby traps.

Once he'd cut the fishing line, Jonas pulled the M44 from the ground by the stake, removed the poisoned capsule, then took everything else apart.

Working carefully, he lifted the new-looking purse off the branch and checked inside. It was empty except for a rock at the bottom—ballast. He dumped out the stone, placed the parts of the device inside, then stuck the purse into his backpack. He'd go over the components later.

"There's a piece of metal over there, just to the left of that shrub," Emily said, pointing. "I saw it flash in the sun when the breeze moved the branches."

Jonas inched forward carefully, probing the ground with the stick. Suddenly there was a loud crunch. Leaves and dust flew up as a big half-circle of jagged metal leaped off the ground, clacking loudly.

"A *bear* trap?" Emily asked, then shuddered.

"Two of them—the smaller one, set off the other. But either of these would have practically cut a leg in half."

"This is crazy. Why would anyone targeting us leave a trap like that behind? It's not discriminating. Anyone could have been injured or killed. What if kids had come up here on a hike, or just to mess around below the bluffs?" She ran a hand through her hair in frustration.

"I wish I could answer that."

"Do you think this might have been Sam's work? He's the only person we've seen around here."

"No. I was able to spot a few boot prints where the leaves were blown away by the whip of those jaws on the traps. The impressions don't match those of a man his size. The person here was taller. Heavier, too."

Jonas took the binoculars out of his backpack and made a more detailed search of the surrounding area. He concentrated on the higher ground, where several large crevices and narrow canyons infiltrated the bluffs, possibly granting a way to the top.

They circled the area for another hour. Although he continued to search for a trail his fellow warrior might have left, in the end, he ran out of time.

"We better head back. The sun's getting low, and we shouldn't be out here after sunset," he said.

"All right. But I want to come back at first light. Someone's playing a deadly game and I want to know who he is and why he's doing this."

"You've got a lot of guts," Jonas stated, glancing over at her in admiration.

She looked at him in surprise. "No, actually I'm scared to death, but this is my *home*. I can't let someone run me off. If I do, I'll be losing far more than my land. I don't think I'd be able to live with myself after that."

It was the simplicity of her words and the powerful sentiment behind them that touched him most. "Facing fear and still doing what's necessary is what courage is all about."

"And you? Are you ever really afraid? You never seem to be."

"That's training. Knowing how to react in any situation makes a lot of difference, but, yeah, I've been scared plenty of times in my life. I don't know of any soldier who hasn't. You just learn not to let it get in the way."

As he led the way back, he chose a roundabout route. They would hike west along high ground first, then return north to the house on a parallel course to the trail they'd followed on the way up. It would also give him one last chance to intercept a trail leading up toward the bluffs from the highway—the most direct route Dinétsoh could have taken from the accident site.

Several hundred yards after they'd turned in the direction of the house, he spotted tracks in the soft dirt. Two distinct sets of footprints were visible leading away from Emily's home.

Jonas crouched down and studied each. Near the first, he could see where drops of blood had fallen onto the rock.

He weighed his options carefully. If he didn't follow the trail now, a windstorm or an unexpected shower could destroy it in a matter of minutes. But under the present circumstances, he couldn't send Emily home on her own.

"If you think we're just going to head back home instead of following that trail, you're nuts," she said. "Those are Dinétsoh's footprints."

"What makes you so sure?" he asked immediately.

"He had a very slight limp. I know, because whenever we'd go out hiking, he'd take the lead. He never liked the Anglo way that required a man to step aside so the woman could walk ahead of him. He said that it made no sense to him. Men had to go first so they could protect their families from danger." She smiled, remembering. "Back in those days, I noticed his tracks reflected the almost imperceptible way he dragged his left leg. Like that," she said, pointing down.

Jonas nodded, already having noted that. "These tracks aren't fresh, so whatever battle was fought here is long finished. But I can't guarantee we won't run into other problems or encounter more danger."

"Did I ask for a guarantee?"

He could have hugged her. "You're terrific," he said, flashing her a grin. "All right then. Let's get going." He stood and readjusted his backpack. "I'll take point."

They followed the tracks for several hundred yards, continuing downhill, and soon came to a damp, sandy wash. The wild grasses were taller here, and long, wavy lines in the sand indicated the direction water had flowed recently.

"This is an intermittent stream," he noted. "He might have crossed here when there was a little water flowing. If he was trying to elude someone, it would have obscured his trail. There were some isolated storms in the area, too, the day before the…incident."

"Water comes and goes here during the rainy season," Emily said, remembering taking long walks back in the days when she hadn't had a care in the world.

"I want to check along the other side of the wash, up and down the flow. It probably won't do much good, but you never know," Jonas mused. "Why don't you wait for me? I can work faster alone and I won't be long." Here, she'd have enough cover to shield her. "If you need me, just yell. I'll hear you."

He returned a short while later and shook his head. "The only trail I found was the one belonging to the person who followed the man with the limp. It looks like he finally gave up and headed back northwest."

She gazed in that direction, shading her eyes from the sun, which was now low in the sky. "The highway's over there, isn't it? In fact, we're only about a mile from where my dad died. Could that first set of tracks have been left by my father? Maybe he took off from the accident site, injured, trying to avoid someone. Then, later, he returned to the car, but passed on before the deputies found him." By some miracle she kept her voice from shaking.

"Does that really fit with what the police told you about the incident?" he asked her gently.

She shook her head and sighed. "No. They said my dad was pinned in—trapped." She took an unsteady breath and, wiping tears away, added, "but something tells me you know more about that than I do."

He'd been briefed by someone who'd been at the accident

scene, but the gruesome details weren't for the ears of a close relative or even a friend. Uncertain of what he could tell her, Jonas kept his eyes on the distance, trying to figure things out. "How tall was your dad?" he asked at last.

"Five foot ten."

"Then neither set of prints belong to him," he said. "I'm five foot nine, and I wear a size twelve. Your father was taller than I am, so I figure he must have worn at least a fourteen." He paused, then in a pensive voice continued. "The only sure thing the trail we've found tells us is that one man, though injured, was mobile. He went across the wash in hopes of hiding his passage. That's how he lost the guy behind him."

"Then Dinétsoh was the one being pursued," she said. "Don't bother to deny it. Although you still haven't given me the missing man's name, it's clear that he was the one with my father the day of the accident."

Jonas had been ordered to withhold information from her, but it was pointless now. "It's true," he said with a nod. "We also suspect that your father and our friend were attacked and run off the highway."

"But those traps. If Dinétsoh has already passed by, why place them there at all?"

"Probably to impede whoever might come looking for him," Jonas answered. "They must have been set fairly recently, too, because my people would have come across them when they were out looking for Dinétsoh."

"But if he's the target, then why is someone coming after me, too? I haven't seen Dinétsoh in years."

"That, I can't answer. But your father plays a part in this, too. Maybe someone believes you know more than you do, or have whatever it is they want."

"I'm not a threat to anyone," she said wearily. "All I want is to build my inn. Why can't I make them see that?"

The tremor in her voice got to him, and without thinking,

he pulled her into his arms. For a brief eternity he held her, rubbing his cheek against her hair and enjoying the softness of her body against his.

"It's hard to predict what they'll do next, but here's one thing you can count on. No one will harm you, not while wind breath remains in me."

Wind breath—what animated the body. Emily knew the term. With a sigh, she snuggled even deeper into his arms.

His whole body responded to her. He needed her—and not just for a one-nighter. That sure knowledge pounded through him. But he had to guard Emily and keep her safe. Emotions would compromise his judgment and that wasn't what she needed from him—or what he expected from himself.

Reluctantly easing his hold, Jonas took a step back, giving himself room to think.

"There's still something you haven't told me," she said as they got under way again. "What makes this parcel of land so special to the tribe? Let's face it, `Anaasází sites are not that uncommon around this area."

Knowing he wasn't at liberty to discuss that with anyone, and opting not to lie to her, he again chose his words carefully.

"The parcel is very close to the Navajo Irrigation Project, southeast of here. It's also an area archeologists have wanted to explore for a long time. As much as possible, the tribe wants to control what goes on near our reservation."

"Grant... Do you think he could have hiked over there and set those traps? If I died, or was incapacitated and unable to make my mortgage payments, I'm sure he'd figure out a way to buy up the land. I don't have any heirs."

"That's one possibility, sure, but I should tell you that Woods has an alibi for the time of your father's car crash. According to the deputies who followed up on the incident, he was fixing the roof on his house with his handyman—Sam Carpenter—at the time."

"Considering what we know about Carpenter, I don't think that's exactly a solid alibi. Money can't buy loyalty, but it can hire liars."

"Even so, we have no way of disproving their alibi or placing them at the scene, not unless a third party comes forward with information. This area is so isolated almost anything can happen without witnesses. But it still doesn't seem likely that Woods would negotiate drilling rights with your father, then kill him. And I'm sure he wouldn't be working so hard to get you to sell if he considered murder an option."

"Those drilling rights… Have you found out if it's possible the contract's a forgery?"

"Experts are checking on that," Jonas said. "I should know something by later this evening."

They arrived at the trailer after sundown and he walked her to the door. "Try to get some sleep and don't worry."

"What about you? Will you be getting some rest?"

"Enough."

"You need sleep, too—unless you've got superpowers I haven't seen."

"Maybe someday I'll show those to you," he said with a thoroughly masculine grin, then wished her good-night.

Once she was safely inside the trailer, he moved away, staying in the shadows. There was one possibility he hadn't broached with her. Her father's accident could have been a move against the Brotherhood itself, and Dinétsoh the only target. Her father's death could amount to nothing more than collateral damage during an assault meant to kidnap or kill a Brotherhood warrior.

Yet that theory didn't explain the acts of vandalism and the attacks against her—unless she'd seen or knew something she wasn't even aware of.

Jonas spat out an oath. He had too many questions and very few answers. He only knew one thing for sure. When the time came for him to move on, he'd be leaving a piece of himself behind.

Refusing to dwell on that now, he reached for his cell phone and reported in.

Chapter Eight

Emily was up by the crack of dawn. The day she'd been looking forward to, and dreading at the same time, had finally arrived. Today, the main house would be demolished, and what had once been her home would give way to the future.

Emily had just turned on the coffeepot when she heard a knock at her trailer door. She answered it and invited Jonas inside.

"It's barely six-thirty. I wasn't sure if you'd be up, but then I saw that your lights were on."

"Today's the big day."

He sat across from her at the small table. "I've got some news," he said. "First, I gave the components of the cyanide trap we encountered yesterday to a specialist. He couldn't find any fingerprints or trace evidence on any of it, including the purse."

"I'm not surprised. Whoever we're after is more careful than that," she said. "Any news on the gas and mineral-rights contract?"

He nodded. "Our expert has determined that your father's signature is undoubtedly a forgery. Though it looks to be an ordinary signature, it's really several carefully drawn, individual strokes, and they don't match up right when examined under a microscope and special lights. On the other hand, Grant Woods's signature is written in smooth, continuous strokes. Our tribal expert believes other forensic authorities will back that up, and you'd have a good chance of winning if you contest it in court. This kind of evidence would be even more damning on the original contract, which Woods probably has."

"The problem is that I don't have the cash to take it to court. My funds are extremely low right now. I have enough to keep things rolling here until the basic structure is finished, but that's about it. I won't be able to pay for the rest of the fixtures and furnishings needed to open up the place, not to mention landscaping, road improvements and such, unless the land sale to the tribe goes through. I know they'll need the bearer bonds before payment can be made, but if the deal's on paper, I might be able to get credit."

"I'm not sure tribal leaders will sign anything—not until they have the bonds in hand," he warned, "but I guess we'll see. Let's go talk to your attorney. If he has the new draft of the contract, we'll take it from there."

"His office opens at nine. That gives us time to fix a decent breakfast. I don't normally eat this early, but pancakes sound good to me right about now."

"Pancakes sound great. Do you have honey or syrup?" Though army food was pretty good, even out in the field, he missed home cooking.

"I've got honey from local hives," Emily said, rising to her feet. "Now, how good of a cook are you?"

BY EIGHT FORTY-FIVE, they were on their way into the city. As she gazed at the tall bluffs to the south, she silently wondered how long she'd be able to see them. The pressure seemed to be taking a toll on her sight. This morning she'd noticed that the dark spot on the lower quadrant of her visual field had widened.

"Don't be in such a rush to get your plans off the ground," he said, misreading her change of mood. "When things are this complicated it can take time to sort everything out."

She didn't answer. How could she explain that she *had* to

get everything finished while she could still see? She wanted to remember every detail of the inn, like the beauty of the sun as it spilled into the rooms that would welcome her guests. The joy of brightness and colors... Those would be only a memory someday.

"Tell me what you're thinking," he said gently.

She hesitated, then spoke. "Although the inn was my dream, my dad made it his, too. That's why it's even more important to me now to see this through. If I let anything stop me, I won't be just failing myself. I'll be failing him, as well," she said. "That's why I won't give up, no matter what anyone throws at me."

That was one of the many reasons Emily had woven a path straight to his heart. The woman didn't know the meaning of surrender—except in his arms. The thought sent a jolt through him.

He drew in his breath, then shifted his attention to something less troublesome. "So what's your construction schedule like after the old house is torn down? You've never given me the details."

"The inn will be built on the site where the main house stands. There'll be extra-wide hallways for wheelchairs, low cabinets and furniture, and special ramps and handholds everywhere, particularly the bathrooms. I also want nature trails set up to accommodate the special needs of my guests. Once it's all finished, I'll memorize every single detail—and celebrate!"

"Celebrate, yes, but why memorize the details? You'll see them every morning when you get up," he said, instantly picking up on what she'd left unsaid.

Thinking fast, Emily tried to cover up for her lapse. "It's at that moment when you see everything finished for the first time that the feeling of accomplishment is the strongest. That's what I'll be pressing into the scrapbook of my mind."

He nodded, unconvinced, but quickly focused back on the road. The San Juan River bridge was just ahead, and such highway features often became squeeze points and danger zones.

"Do you keep scrapbooks?" she asked as they turned east into town. "I'd bet anything that you have a trunk full of medals and commendations."

"I have them," he said. "They're in the closet in a box. Someday I'll probably look at them again, but for now, I'd rather put some distance between me and those memories."

His words held a rawness that nearly broke her heart. "I'm sorry. I didn't mean to pry. I was only thinking of the pride you must have felt in a job well done."

"The job got done, but sometimes at the expense of our dearest blood," he said, his voice flat. "Remember the saying 'what doesn't kill you will make you stronger'? It was like that for most of us."

Following the whispers of her heart, Emily reached for his hand, intertwining her fingers through his. He squeezed her hand in response, but said nothing.

Even as the minutes ticked by and they entered the city, he didn't let go. Ribbons of warmth spiraled through her as she realized that he needed her. An undeniable peace settled over her. It was like discovering that the wind needed the sound it made through the trees in order to remember its passage.

Shutting out everything but the present, she leaned back, looked at people on the sidewalks and allowed herself the luxury of enjoying the moment. For now, she'd bask in the simple pleasure of holding hands.

"Starting an inn in our depressed economy is a risky thing," he said, finding a parking place near the downtown civic center. "Have you considered that?"

"Sure, but I'll be catering to a clientele most places overlook. What I'll have to offer won't be unique, but my guests will appreciate it," she said confidently as she climbed out of the pickup.

And more important, she would have found a new way to define herself. Being an innkeeper who catered to people with special needs appealed to her on every imaginable level.

As they walked down the sidewalk in the direction of Robert Jefferson's office, Jonas kept an eye out for problems, making certain no one in a passing vehicle or on the sidewalk sent off any warning signs.

"I've been thinking about your cash-flow problems. Once the drilling rights question is settled, there may be a way for the tribe to guarantee you credit. You could sign a contract agreeing not to sell that land to anyone but us," he said. "The tribe wants that parcel, so I think they'd work with you, particularly if it means they have extra time to come up with the money."

"That's a good idea," she said. "But I'm still trying to understand your explanation about why the tribe wants it. There are zoning laws, but other than that, you can't really control what happens on land adjacent to yours, no matter how many parcels you buy. Eventually, someone on the other side of the property line will do something you don't like. It's not as if it hasn't happened before."

He had to give her credit; she knew there was something he'd left unsaid, and wasn't willing to let it go until she got the whole story. No wonder she'd gotten under his skin. Emily was everything he'd ever wanted in a woman and more. She was ice and flame. She was all cool logic when she needed to be. Yet in his arms she was pure fire.

He'd sworn to keep his distance, but running away wasn't his style. And that was the problem in a nutshell. Yet, deep in his gut, he knew he had to let her go. She needed more than someone like him could give her.

As they waited at a stoplight, he came up with a way to answer her. "Undeveloped land like yours, with access to water and electricity, phones and the like, is at a premium. The added plus in this case is that it could also be used for agricultural purposes. All that, and the fact that it contains pieces of our past and our culture, makes it of great interest to us."

"And that's all?" she pressed.

No one had ever been able to read him like Emily could. She knew he hadn't told her everything. Minutes passed and he heard her sigh.

"I'm not going to let it go," she told him.

"I know."

They arrived at the attorney's office a few minutes later. Jen Caldwell, the petite, buxom assistant, greeted them with a hesitant smile. "I'm sorry, Ms. Atkins, but Mr. Jefferson isn't here. Is there something I can do to help you?"

Emily told her why they'd come. "Robert was supposed to get the new contract ready for me. Do you know if he did?"

"I have no idea, but let me check your file."

Jen stepped away from her desk and went into Robert's office. She returned a few minutes later empty-handed. "I couldn't find anything in his file cabinet or on his desktop computer. But he's got his laptop with him. That's usually where he keeps files pertaining to current work."

"Could you give him a call for us?" Emily pressed.

"I've been trying to get hold of him for an hour, but he's not answering. I've tried his BlackBerry and his home phone, too. He has meetings scheduled for this afternoon, so he's bound to check in sooner or later. When he does, I'll tell him you stopped by and wanted to speak to him."

"Can you give us his other telephone numbers?" Jonas asked.

"No, I'm sorry. That's strictly against our policy, but I'll leave him a text and voice message regarding your visit."

As they left the office, Jonas was quiet. "I think I can find out where Robert lives," he murmured at last. "If I do, what do you say we go over to his house?"

"Sounds good to me," she answered.

A cold breeze blew against them, and seeing her shiver, he placed his arm around her shoulder. Without even thinking about it, she leaned into him. The warmth and safety he offered were addictive. But reminding herself that he was only a war-time ally, and once the peace was restored, he'd be gone, gave her strength to move away.

Jonas made the call, and within ten minutes they were heading east out of the city. The attorney's home was located in a neighborhood filled with high-end housing near the country club. Yet despite the size of each of the homes, they were on small tracts of land, and that gave the neighborhood a closed-in feel.

They found the house using Jonas's GPS, and parked at the curb near the front door. "The newspaper's still on his front step," Jonas said, as they approached the porch. "And there's mail in the box, maybe two days' worth. It doesn't look like anyone's been here recently."

They walked around and listened at the windows, but no sounds came from inside the house, and the curtains were drawn.

Emily turned back toward their car, and saw a neighbor watching them from across the street. "Uh-oh, we've got somebody's attention."

"Smile and wave, Emily," Jonas whispered, then brought out his wallet and flashed a badge in the direction of the woman. "I'm Security," he yelled. "Have you seen Mr. Jefferson today, ma'am?"

"Not since yesterday. And his car wasn't in the driveway this morning," the woman called back.

"Thank you," Jonas replied. "Time to go," he whispered to Emily, motioning toward the pickup.

"What's with the badge? I didn't know you had one."

"It's for show—not tell," he said with a grin.

They left quickly before the woman could ask any questions, and were well down the street before Emily spoke again. "If no car's been around, maybe he never came home. We saw him just yesterday, right? I hope he hasn't decided to leave town all of a sudden."

"Let me check into that and see what I can find out," Jonas

said. It was possible that their visit, and the revelation that Grant Woods was trying to undercut the sale to the tribe—and Jefferson's commission—explained the attorney's sudden absence.

Jonas pulled over to the side of the road and made a quick call to Diné Nééz. Speaking in their native tongue, he updated his contact, Jonas giving him the name of what he believed to be Robert Jefferson's cell-phone carrier, based upon an envelope he'd noticed on the assistant's desk.

While waiting for a response, Jonas glanced over at Emily. "Your attorney could be working against your interests. He might be trying to cut a better deal for himself with Woods."

"What would he use as a bargaining point?"

"He could agree to tell you that the gas and mineral rights contract is legit, and leverage himself to take a cut of that pie."

"If that's what he's doing, I'll make sure everyone in the community knows him for the crook he is."

Jonas turned away as Diné Nééz came back on the line.

"We'll call our contact at the cell-phone carrier," he announced. "Maybe we can pick up his GPS location."

One advantage the Brotherhood had was that they could cut corners modern law enforcement couldn't.

While finishing his conversation, Jonas heard Emily's cell phone ring. A few moments later, he clicked off and focused on her. "What's going on?" he asked, reading trouble in her expression.

"More bad news. I just got a call from Ken, the construction foreman. The access road leading to both my property and Grant Woods's land is now blocked at the highway. Several gas-company employees and their vehicles, including a backhoe, are parked in the way. The men are claiming they have utility work to complete alongside the highway, and that Ken'll have to wait."

"And he doesn't want to?"

"The problem is he rented some heavy equipment and delays

are going to be costly. He could send everything back, but he'd still have to pay, and it may be several days before he can get the equipment again. Even if he decides to sit there and wait it out, he'll still have to pay his men. That'll ultimately come out of my pocket, too."

"Is there an alternate route they could take to your place?" Jonas asked.

Emily shook her head. "Not without knocking down several big cottonwoods. An easier way would be tearing down the fence and going through Grant Woods's property. Unfortunately, his gate is locked and nobody seems to be home."

"Do you have his number?"

She nodded. "I tried calling, but no one answers. He probably wouldn't give us permission, anyway, especially after what happened last time we spoke to him."

"This just seems to be our lucky day," Jonas muttered. Someone was trying to push their buttons. But no one played *him*. "Let's go back to your home. Maybe we can convince the gas company to clear a path."

They arrived less than fifteen minutes later. Parked along the shoulder of the highway just before the turnoff to her property were four vehicles. Two were pickups, and the others, tractor trailers hauling a backhoe and small bulldozer. The construction workers, including her foreman, were pacing impatiently by their vehicles.

About twenty feet in from the shoulder of the road were bright orange construction cones blocking access. Beyond, five men were standing in front of a dump truck, which towed a trailer hauling a backhoe. Two white gas company pickups were parked beside the barrier.

Emily waved at her foreman as Jonas drove past, pulling up in front of the cones.

A big man in the gas company's tan trousers and shirt, wearing a bright yellow vest and hard hat, came over immediately.

"You can't park here, sir. We're checking a gas line for leaks. Better turn around, because we're going to be here for hours." The spokesman, whose name tag read Michaels, motioned toward another employee walking along the fence line with a sensing instrument.

"I don't smell any gas. Who reported the leak?" Jonas asked, stepping out of the truck.

"I don't know. The field service office dispatched us."

Emily crossed in front of the vehicle and stood beside Jonas. Three other men in coveralls, carrying large shovels, moved toward them.

"Just give us five minutes," she said quickly, hoping to avoid more trouble. "I live down that road and my foreman has construction equipment that needs to go through." She kept her tone neutral, opting for a rational approach.

"Sorry, lady—too dangerous. Now clear the area. Tell your foreman that this could very well take all day, so they might as well head back to the yard."

She was determined to keep her temper in check, but the man's attitude plain irked her. "I want to see your work order," Emily demanded, stepping up to the man and staring up into his face. She was five-seven, but he had a height advantage of at least a foot.

"Sorry—in an emergency the paperwork comes later."

"Bull," Jonas growled. He'd enjoyed seeing her challenge the tree trunk in front of her. That fiery determination of hers was something else. But she needed backup, and that's why he was here. "You get a call, you get a job order, even for a safety check. Produce it for the lady now, or put away your gear and take off." He stepped up within a foot of the man, his eyes hard.

"Back off," one of the oncoming workers snapped.

Jonas sized up Big Mouth instantly. He looked like a body builder with a steroid hangover. The gorilla was carrying a shovel at quarter arms, more like a rifle than a digging implement.

Jonas reached out and, with lightning fast reflexes, grabbed the shovel, pushing and twisting at the same time. The big man struggled, but lost the fight.

As he staggered back, he spat out an oath, then lunged at Jonas like a stampeding bull.

Jonas turned his side to the charge and stepped back at the last second. The man crashed into the front of their truck, then whirled around, his fists up.

Emily stepped between them, holding her arms out in both directions. "Stop!"

She looked from Jonas to the gas company men who were moving in closer now, ready for a fight. "Everyone needs to calm down and start acting civilized."

"Step out of the way, Em," Jonas said, his voice a deadly purr, his eyes hard and gleaming like flint.

"Having trouble, Emily?" A voice came from up the road. It was her foreman, Ken, and three of his men were directly behind him.

Emily knew that in another second, all hell would break loose. Somehow, she had to keep this from escalating. "Hang on a minute, Ken."

She faced the gas company's foreman and raised her cell phone. "All right, Mr. Michaels. Who do you suggest I call first—the sheriff, or maybe Channel 4? Oh, I know. If I call the law, I'll get both, since the reporters will pick up the incident on their police scanners."

"Just hold on there, Ms. Atkins. There's no need for this to become some sort of incident. We're just trying to track down a leak." He turned to the man who held the sensor. "Any readings, Bob?"

Bob was slow on the uptake, and didn't respond until one of his colleagues jabbed him in the ribs, shaking his head simultaneously.

"Uh, no," he finally replied.

"Good call, Bob," Jonas said, crossing his arms and leaning

back against the hood of his truck. "Guess you gentlemen can pack up now and leave. You might check back down the road toward town. I think I smelled something funky when we crossed the bridge."

The men backed off, but the muscle-bound weight lifter turned to Jonas and pointed.

"Oh, I forgot—your shovel." He tossed the implement, and the man had to jump to catch it.

Five minutes later the gas company vehicles were on their way, heading toward town.

"That's too bad," Jonas said as he watched them leave. "It would have been fun to mix it up a little."

Ken nodded. "I've got to say, I'm a bit disappointed myself."

"Hey, maybe they'll come back, boss," one of the construction workers called out.

Emily glared at them, threw her hands in the air and climbed back into the truck.

"You were all kidding back there, right?" she asked when Jonas joined her.

He shrugged and gave her a playful half smile. "But I've got to say, I was impressed with your style. All things considered, I'd rather tangle with Michaels than have a face-off with you."

"I was trying to keep all of you from getting hurt!"

"You were something to watch—dark eyes staring daggers at the guy, skin flushed. Just beautiful!"

"You beast!"

Before she could say anything else he pulled her toward him and kissed her hard. All he'd wanted to do was quiet her, but the minute his mouth covered hers, fire spread through him.

Hearing her whimper as his tongue danced with hers made a surge of heat blast through him. He'd never wanted anyone or anything more than he wanted Emily at that very moment.

Hearing a knock on the driver's side window, he cursed the interruption, and reluctantly pulled away.

"What?" he growled, staring at Ken.

The foreman grinned. "We'll follow you in?"

"Yeah," Jonas snapped, then switched on the ignition. "The road's clear now. Give your crew the go-ahead."

"What was that really about—with those gas-company people?" Emily asked, trying hard to forget the way his kiss had made her feel. The surprise, the passion behind it, had left her stunned—and what's worse, wanting more. "Was that just another attempt to slow up the project?"

"I think so," he said. "Who else might know you're short on funds?"

"The people at the bank, I suppose, but I don't make my finances public."

"Your real-estate attorney knows your finances down to the last dollar, probably—the one who was conveniently unavailable today," Jonas added thoughtfully. "How much do you really know about Jefferson?"

"Not much, except that Dad knew him, and he's the only real-estate attorney in this area."

"What about Woods? What kind of work does he do?"

"Grant's a CPA. Sometimes he takes on work for the county, but mostly he's self-employed. Why?"

"I'm trying to figure out who might have hired those men."

"According to the signs on the trucks, and their uniforms, they were from the gas company."

Jonas shook his head. "The signs look real enough, but they were the magnetic stick-on kind. The gas company paints their logos in place. My guess is that those men were hired by someone who wanted to slow down your construction and set you back another few thousand bucks. That guy Michaels—it probably wasn't even his shirt."

Jonas parked by her trailer. "I need to go look into a few things, but you'll have plenty of backup nearby," he said, gesturing to Ken and his men, who'd come in right behind them.

"Go do what you have to. I can handle things here," she said firmly.

"You're a strong woman who doesn't like to depend on anyone. I get it, Em. I really do," Jonas said. "But working as part of a team increases the odds in your favor. In times of trouble, each person brings something to the mix—one more asset that helps complete a successful mission. Being able to stand on your own two feet is important, but so's using your support."

After she climbed out of the cab, he drove slowly past the construction crew, who were already hustling to get started, lowering the ramps on their equipment trailers. Recognizing a member of the Brotherhood among the workers, Jonas gave him a nod, and drove on.

He was halfway to the highway when he saw another pickup parked by the side of the road. Diné Nééz was leaning against the driver's side, waiting, as if he'd been expecting Jonas.

That was impossible, of course. Jonas had only made the decision to contact him and arrange to meet a few minutes earlier. Yet, there he was.

"*Yáat'ééh,* nephew," Diné Nééz said as Jonas pulled up alongside.

"*Yáat'ééh,* Uncle," he answered. Though there was no kinship between them, the term *uncle* denoted respect.

"You handled the problem with the gas company well," he stated.

"You saw?" Seeing him nod, Jonas glanced down at the now-empty road. "I'm sure the whole thing was staged—another attempt to stall the construction project."

"Since your call earlier, we've been trying to find that real-estate attorney, Jefferson. We've had no luck."

"The stakes are high for Ms. Atkins. Though he has no clear motive except the desire to buy the land, her neighbor, Grant Woods, concerns me."

Diné Nééz nodded. "We're checking into his finances to get

a clearer picture of him. But watch your back. Our enemies are more numerous than we believed at first."

Jonas drove back toward Emily's place, still trying to figure out how he had known about the confrontation with the utility people so quickly. Maybe the Brotherhood warrior who was a member of the construction team had phoned in a report.

Yet even so, Jonas had a feeling Diné Nééz hadn't been far, and had come in after that to gather his own intelligence. The ability to be there when needed, and gone the next, characterized the Brotherhood's entire mission.

As Jonas returned to the site, stopping long enough to allow the workers to back the bulldozer off the big trailer, his thoughts once again centered on Emily. Something more than funding lay at the root of her fears, and one way or another, he was going to find out what that was and help her through it.

Destiny had brought Emily back into his life, maybe to remind him of love, and it was that same feeling that would eventually force him to leave her behind. Her long-term safety would demand his absence. But before he left, he'd complete what he'd set out to do. He'd restore harmony so she could walk in beauty. It would be a fitting, parting gift to the woman he loved.

Chapter Nine

Emily paced inside the trailer. She'd never really gotten over Jonas. But what continued to draw her to him was more than the brief past they'd shared. Faced with the man he'd become, she found her feelings for him had deepened—and that was the problem. Life had taught her that love couldn't be trusted. Her mother had seemed happy at home, yet one day she'd left them without warning. No amount of love had been able to hold her.

It would be that way with Jonas someday, too. His nature demanded freedom, not emotional commitments.

The only person she could ultimately depend on was herself. Trying not to think of the lonely road ahead, she went outside and watched as the crew demolished her father's old house. The bulldozer made quick work of the walls, then continued its assault, grinding the roof into rubble.

Her chest tightened as she watched her past being reduced to dust. She missed her father—his love and his support. When she'd needed him most, he'd been there for her. His strength had held her up and given her courage. Now he was gone, too. She wiped away the tear that ran down her face.

"Are you all right?"

She hadn't heard Jonas come up, and his voice made her jump. Emily quickly scrubbed any moisture from her face and turned around.

"Just saying goodbye to the past," she said, and forced a smile. "I've got so many plans! First the inn will go up. Then I'll build my own private residence right over there, where my mom had planned to build her workshop," she said, pointing. "That old concrete pad will be torn up and a new foundation laid."

"How big will you make your home—three or four bedrooms?"

"It'll be one bedroom with a small office. I want a cozy house, not a large one," she said. "Actually, it won't be much larger than the place my mom had in mind."

"What kind of hobby did your mother have?"

"She was an avid quilter. Mom spent months and months designing the work space she'd planned for herself, She had everything figured out, down to the shelves," Emily said with a sad smile. "But we never got beyond pouring the concrete foundation."

"Did you ever find out what happened to her?" he asked in a gentle voice.

"No. Everything had been perfectly normal, and we were all excited about the upcoming construction. Then the day before the slab was poured, she just disappeared." Emily's voice was heavy. "Her car was discovered in town, parked just a block from the bus station. But no one there remembered her face, and passengers on the bus usually pay in cash, so there was no trail. Her purse was gone, along with a few hundred dollars she'd set aside to buy shelves."

Emily stared at the concrete pad, lost in thought. "The sheriff's department and Farmington police looked into it, but eventually concluded that she'd taken off on us," she said finally. "At the time they were hot on the trail of another woman, a young housekeeper who'd gone missing a week earlier. They believed that woman had been kidnapped. Since there was no evidence of a crime here, that other case took precedence."

Jonas watched her. Dignity was mirrored in her eyes, and beyond that, something irreparably broken.

"Picking up the pieces of your life after something like that must have been very hard."

"It was. Dad was never the same. He'd hole up in his home office or his workshop. I got involved in school activities, trying to stay busy and keep my mind off things at home. After I left for college, I always found reasons not to come back. It wasn't until a few months ago that things changed between Dad and me."

"What brought that about?" Jonas watched her reaction, noting that the second he asked the question, she stiffened, almost as if startled that she'd spoken so freely. As the seconds stretched out, he had the definite impression that she was mentally scrambling for a reply.

Finally she spoke. "I told Dad about my plans to build an inn and he suggested I come home and do that here. He'd been looking for a new investment that would see him through retirement, and I needed a partner, so I took him up on it."

His time in the Brotherhood and the military before that had taught Jonas to sense omissions. That instinct kicked in strongly now. He was certain that Emily had left out a critical part of her story. Under ordinary circumstances he wouldn't have intruded on her privacy, but the situation was far from normal.

What you didn't know could get you killed. He thought of his Navajo buddy, Marc Atcitty. Marc had been questioning a young boy he'd spotted following their patrol through the village. But, distracted by gunfire from another direction, he'd let the kid go—without patting him down first. Seconds later the boy, a suicide bomber, had detonated his explosive vest, killing Marc and two other Rangers. One moment of omission or carelessness—that's all it took to claim a life.

No matter what it took, Jonas intended to find out what Emily was so determined to keep from him. He'd bring all his resources to bear, and before long, he'd know everything there was to know about her.

As her phone rang, she reached into her pocket. "I placed an ad for some of the antiques I inherited. It was a way to raise a little cash. Hopefully, this'll be a buyer."

She flipped it open. "Yes, the Hoosier cabinet is still available," she said.

Jonas moved away, trying to make up his mind how to go about finding the answers he needed about Emily. Only half aware of her conversation, he looked off into the distance.

"Jonas?"

He glanced back at her, wondering what he'd missed.

"Could you help me move some things away from the Hoosier cabinet in the metal storage compartment? I've got an interested buyer, and I need to answer a question about the spice rack."

"Sure. Let's go."

They walked over to the unit, and after she removed the padlock, walked inside.

"There it is, behind the mantel," she said, pointing.

They made their way among the fixtures, furniture and appliances stored there, and managed to reach it a moment later.

"Blast! The sliding doors are stuck." Emily tugged hard on both brass knobs, but nothing happened.

"Let me see if I can give you a hand," he said, moving past her.

He gave the knobs a good yank, then shook his head. "They didn't even move. Let me get a flashlight and see if there's something jammed in the track."

As he moved away, she stood on tiptoe, then yanked the left-hand knob hard. The entire oak cabinet suddenly wobbled, then started to come down on her. Jonas was there in an instant, holding it in place with both arms, straining from the weight.

Emily tried to push it upright, but the cabinet was heavy and there was very little room for maneuvering.

"I've got it," Jonas rasped. "Move away and go get help."

When she tried to step back, the cabinet wobbled again. "If

either of us moves, this thing will topple on whoever's left behind. The front casters came off, and it won't stay put no matter what."

In as loud a voice as she could muster, she cried out for help, but the noise of the bulldozer drowned her out.

"Move away!" Jonas grunted.

"No." Though her arms were trembling from the effort, she refused to let go. She glanced desperately around the metal storage unit. "I can't see where the casters fell, but I've got an idea. I'm going to have to let go for just a second."

He followed her gaze. "I see your plan. Go for it," Jonas said, sweat forming on his forehead.

She moved away, quickly picked up a section of crown molding, and jammed the piece underneath the oak unit, using it as a brace. Despite the strain, Jonas's arms had remained as steady as steel posts, and his shoulders like rock.

She picked up a second section of molding and placed it on the other side, wedging it in place. "Slack off a little and see if it holds."

Jonas relaxed the pressure and saw that nothing moved. "Good work," he said, stepping back. "Now let's find those casters."

"Somebody in trouble?" Ken called, appearing at the door.

"Nice timing," Emily said, laughing. "But as long as you're here we could use some help."

IT WAS LATE AFTERNOON when she sat across from Jonas at the small table in the trailer. "We were set up with that big cabinet. The caller left me a phoney telephone number, and Ken found that the doors had been glued shut with contact cement. Wood shims had also been placed along the bottom in the back so it was already leaning forward, and the casters removed, then propped in place. The caller was hoping I'd pull the whole thing down on myself."

"You could have been badly injured if that thing *had* come crashing down," Jonas muttered, running an exasperated hand through his hair. "You should have left to go get Ken or one of the other men."

"No. By the time I came back with help, that Hoosier could have crushed you. You needed backup right then. You take care of me, I take care of you. Isn't that the way soldiers work?"

"You're not a soldier," he snapped.

"I'm also not the kind of person who abandons a friend," she said, her voice barely audible. Turning away from him, she went to the sink.

He came up behind her and, pressing his body to hers, whispered in her ear, "You scared the hell out of me, Em. Promise me you won't do something crazy like that again."

Following an instinct she couldn't acknowledge in words, she leaned back into him. "I can't promise you that, but I trust you to do whatever's necessary to keep us both safe."

"Don't trust me so much, Em," Jonas said, and turned her around in his arms. Not giving her a chance to think, he lowered his mouth to hers and drank in her sweetness, needing her softness and wanting to drown himself in her taste.

Emily gasped and shivered as he trailed light kisses down the column of her throat. When he lowered his hand to the swell of her breast, she arched into him.

Knowing that she needed him made him crazy. "Em, what am I going to do with you?" he groaned. "You're a part of me—you owned my dreams. You were the softness that saw me through all those sleepless nights when I was deployed overseas."

The way he cupped her breast, tugging at her nipple, made her mindless with desire. "I never forgot—" she began, then drew in her breath as he squeezed the tip between his thumb and forefinger.

Feeling her melt against him shattered his restraint. Jonas lifted her up into his arms, then carried her to the bed just down the short passage.

"In your arms...there's magic," she said, struggling not to

whisper the secret locked away in her heart. *Love...* That wasn't something that could be spoken aloud between them.

Setting her down on top of the mattress, he lay over her and kissed her again, loving the way she clung to him. He wanted to give her pleasure, to feel her come apart beneath him.

"There's never been anyone else," she whispered, the words torn from her heart.

It was that admission that finally broke him. He would take care of her—and that meant that he wouldn't make love to her. The ties between them were too strong as it was. But he could give her pleasure, and carry the sweet sound of her cries inside him for the rest of his life.

Jonas unfastened the snap of her jeans and slid his hands downward.

"No, we can't," she whispered.

"Will you trust me?" he murmured. "Surrender to me, if only for now."

Without waiting, he moved his hand down until he found the center of her womanhood. Parting the sweet folds, he stroked her gently.

She drew in a breath as sensations too powerful to resist coursed through her. "I..."

"Feel," he murmured. "Don't think."

He caressed her, slowly bringing her to the edge. Drowning in pleasure, she clung to him, the fire at her center too strong to resist. She cried out his name, whimpering and begging for release.

As the late-afternoon sun streamed through a crack in the curtains and bathed her in its golden glow, she shattered against him. He felt her heat, and held her as she came apart, helpless to resist him.

Slowly her breathing evened and she nuzzled against him, needing his strength to find her own again. He held her, sharing in the peace that settled over her as she drifted back to earth.

"*Sawe,*" he whispered. "*Ayóó ninshné.*"

The rough timbre of his voice reverberated against her cheek, which was pressed to his chest. There'd be time to ask what the words meant later. For now, she'd bask in the glow and rest in the shelter of his arms.

IT SEEMED LIKE AN eternity before she could find the energy to move. "I…"

Suddenly embarrassed about what she'd allowed to happen, Emily refused to look at Jonas as she got up and quickly fastened her clothing.

"What's wrong?" he asked gently.

"You gave me so much…but you didn't…"

Jonas went to her and, tilting her head upward, gazed into her eyes. "Giving a woman pleasure satisfies a man, too, *sawe.*"

"What's that mean?"

"*Sweetheart* or *darling* are the closest words in English."

"And the other words you said?"

"They meant…*passion*," he stated, and was glad when she accepted the answer. His words had meant far more than that, and had come straight from his heart, but he'd had no right to voice them.

Still feeling self-conscious, Emily finished dressing quickly and left the small bedroom area.

"It's quiet outside," she said, looking through the kitchen window.

The bulldozer operator was taking off his jacket, and another worker was spraying water from a hose to settle the dust. They were the only ones still around, and they'd be leaving in a few minutes.

"I guess there wasn't time to begin staking out the foundation and putting up any of the wooden forms. Ken said he wanted to do that and the ground plumbing all in the same day. The delay earlier must have made that impossible."

Jonas sat down on the bench-style seat. "Em, we need to talk.

Your attorney has disappeared. I've tried to track him down using our sources, but we've had no luck. Until he surfaces again we need to concentrate on Grant Woods. For whatever reason, he really wants this property, and he also has the financial resources to hire thugs to create problems for you."

She nodded. "I know, and though I can't prove it unless I go to court, you and I both know he forged my dad's signature on that drilling rights contract."

"Since the tribe and you both have a vested interest in this, let me ask and see if they're willing to provide you with another attorney—pro bono."

"Thanks, but no. I'd still like to pay for any attorney services. Do you think they'd be willing to subtract the fee from the purchase price?"

Jonas recognized pride, and knew it was important to Emily to carry her own weight. "Let's see what can be worked out. In the meantime, let's follow up with the county records office. I'm no lawyer, but I'm thinking that if that contract wasn't officially filed and notarized, it might not hold up in court, anyway. Your father's signature was forged, so the document number might not be valid, either. It bears checking out." He glanced at his watch again. "The county office closes at five, so if we leave now, we should be able to make it."

"Let's go," she said.

Jonas hurried with her out to his truck. The shade from the old cottonwood trees was heavy as they crossed the grounds, and he noticed the way she tried to look from the side, using her peripheral vision as she picked her path. Aware of how hard she was concentrating, he suddenly wondered if her vision problems were greater than she'd led him to believe.

"What gave you the idea to build an inn that caters to the handicapped?" he asked, playing a hunch as they climbed into his truck.

"I saw that there was a need for it, and I felt a special kinship to people with disabilities," she said. "Those who succeed do so through determination and by demanding more from themselves. Determination defines them—not their handicaps," she declared, then in a soft voice, added, "Courage, the kind that can move mountains, often works in the dark, and lives behind a wall of silence."

Emily's words stayed in his mind, replaying as he drove rapidly down the dirt road toward the highway. He'd heard a whisper of something beyond her words…maybe the secret that she was fighting so hard to keep from him.

He forced himself to concentrate on the road ahead, rushing to beat the clock. The sun, low in the sky, filtered through the trees in bright flashes, the nearly random patterns making it difficult to see anything but backlit objects.

Halfway around the turn, Jonas reached up to adjust the sun visor, and suddenly spotted a big object on the road. Cursing under his breath, he braked hard and swerved to the left. As he did, the driver's side of the truck dropped and the left tire sank down into a hole. The truck plowed ahead, shaking like a wet dog.

"Hang on," he called, fighting the wheel.

The truck fishtailed, dipping even lower on the driver's side as they hit a pocket of sand. Fighting hard to avoid a rollover, Jonas yanked the steering wheel back to the right, and the pickup slid to a stop, tilted at a steep angle.

Chapter Ten

Emily gulped in a lungful of air as he switched off the ignition. "What happened?" she managed to ask, her voice shaky. "Was there an animal in the road?"

He unbuckled his seat belt and glanced over at her. She hadn't seen it... Had she been looking the other way, daydreaming? Or was there more to it?

"I swerved to avoid a fallen branch, but the shoulder of the road on my side caved in and I had to fight to keep us from rolling. Maybe one of the dump-truck loads collapsed a culvert. Let's go take a look. Hopefully, we're not stuck."

"Are you sure it's safe to get out? The pickup's really at an angle now," she said, staying very still.

"It's not steep enough to tip over, but you'll need to get out on my side, where you'll be a lot closer to the ground. Just be careful where you put your feet. We're halfway down an embankment."

He got out then, taking her hand to steady her, and helped her out of the pickup. She moved carefully, relying more on him than her own view of the ground. Knowing that she had trouble seeing in low light, he led her around the truck to the road.

"Will you be okay here?" he asked.

"Sure. Go ahead and do whatever you have to."

Jonas stepped back to check out his truck. "The tire looks okay, but the wheel's half buried in the sand. I'm going to dig out that tire, make a trench it can follow, then put some brush in front and around the rear tires to get some traction. If I don't, the tires will just spin and dig in deeper," he said, crouching by the front of the truck.

"I hear a car," she said, as he was reaching behind the backseat for a small shovel. "Someone's coming in from the highway."

Their accident, followed by a driver coming up at just the right time on a private road, was like a warning flag in his brain. Stalkers often set up "rescues" for their potential victims.

"Come around to this side and keep the engine compartment between you and the upcoming vehicle," he said, positioning himself between Emily and the possible threat.

As he waited, braced for whatever came, Jonas could feel the weight of the gun and holster beneath his jacket, out of view but not out of reach.

It was now dark enough for vehicles with sensors to have their headlamps switched on, and within a few seconds he saw the bright lights of a familiar tan crew cab. The upscale model pulled up just ahead of them and stopped.

Grant Woods stepped out and came around the open door, looking over the hood of the big pickup. "Trouble just seems to find you two, doesn't it?" he commented. "I'd offer to help you dig out, but I don't have a shovel. Carpenter's using it while working on the fence line."

He glanced at Emily, who was barely visible on the other side of Jonas's pickup. "Emily, would you like me to drive you home? Or you could come to my house for something warm to drink. With the sun setting soon, and the breeze starting to pick up, it's getting cold out here."

"No, thanks. I'm fine," Emily answered, her voice calm and detached.

"Okay, then. Just thought I'd offer." Grant climbed back in and drove off, accelerating quickly enough to add a cloud of dust to their situation.

Coughing, Emily moved closer to Jonas, who was watching the taillights as her neighbor raced away. The turnoff to his property was just a few hundred yards farther, and the gate automatically opened just ahead of his truck.

"I've never really liked him, and on some level I think he knows it. Yet it doesn't seem to phase him," Emily said.

"I've seen his kind before. They're basically lonely people who haven't got a clue how to make friends. A woman smiles at them, and all of a sudden they're in love—or obsessed."

Jonas reached into the pickup and brought out a powerful flashlight. It was too dim now to pick out any prominent marks without extra lighting.

He moved to where the big branch lay across the center of the road, stopped and looked around. The closest cottonwood was a hundred feet or more away, and no limbs extended over the road, or even close.

Lost in thought, he returned to where they'd run off the road. The hole where the tire had broken through still contained soft, dry sand, though the surrounding roadbed was packed almost rock hard.

The person who'd placed the log on the road had no doubt engineered their accident. The lowlife had dug out a hole in the hard-packed surface, then filled the pit with sand. In the flashlight beam, he could make out the imprints of a pick around the edges of the crater.

Searching at the side of the road, he found shovel marks and a cavity where sand had been carried over to fill the hole. There was also a pile of road-hardened clods. The perp, or perps, had taken care to smooth out any footprints with a shovel. The work had been done quickly, probably after the last of the construction workers had passed by.

As he glanced over at Emily, he saw her rubbing her eyes. "Are you sure you're okay?"

"Yeah, but it looks like we're going to be here awhile. I won't be much help digging unless you have a second shovel and a big lantern."

"No second shovel," he answered. Though he was still curious about the problem with her eyes, this wasn't the time to bring it up. He had other pressing business at the moment, like digging them out before it got totally dark.

LONG AFTER HE'D DROPPED Emily off at her trailer, Jonas drove to a high spot on her property. It was past midnight by the time he met with Diné Nééz.

"I need more background on the woman you've assigned me to protect," he said, his voice low and direct.

Diné Nééz sat on the ground, lost in thought and aimlessly tracing something on the soft earth with a stick.

Knowing that other warriors were watching over Emily, Jonas didn't feel pressed for time. He waited, studying the stars.

"Do you feel it?" Diné Nééz asked at last. "This isn't our land, not according to the white man's law, but even here, outside our borders, the sacred mountains in the distance watch over us."

After spending so much of the last decade outside the rez, Jonas wasn't sure how much to believe anymore. He was *alní*, cut in half between his heritage and the hard lessons learned living the life of a Ranger. Yet the modern-day warrior within him wasn't easily pacified, and his spirit demanded more than the old stories for strength to continue the fight. What kept him going was an unflagging dedication to restoring order. He knew he could make a difference here.

"I have all the information you need," Diné Nééz said, interrupting his thoughts. "That family has had many tragedies."

"Why wasn't I given a complete profile during my briefing?" he demanded.

"It wasn't considered necessary at the time," the warrior answered. Another minute went by before he continued. "When the attorney's daughter was still in high school, she left town on a weekend field trip to Mesa Verde, taking a bus directly from school. The mother disappeared sometime that same day—a Friday, according to law enforcement records."

"What about her father? Where was he during this time?"

"He'd been working on a delicate matter for us and was in Arizona. He returned home on Saturday when he couldn't reach his wife on the phone Friday evening. A concrete slab had been poured on Friday afternoon, but all the construction workers there at the time agreed that Mrs. Atkins hadn't been at home when they did the job."

"Did the Brotherhood join the search to find her?"

"Yes, we did so at the attorney's request, but there was no trail to follow. Her car was found in the city, close to the bus station. It appeared to be a clear case of abandonment, particularly in view of a statement made by Grant Woods, the son of their neighbor."

"What was his involvement?"

"Nothing direct. He went on record telling the sheriff that he'd seen Mrs. Atkins meeting a man outside the public library several times, but the description he gave didn't lead to a suspect. Local authorities checked out security cameras in the library area, but found nothing they could use. The case was eventually set aside for lack of leads. At the time, too, the police were busy working another missing person's case, and they already had a suspect."

"Did they ever cross-check to see if that suspect had a connection to Mrs. Atkins?" Jonas asked, always suspicious of seemingly coincidental events.

"No, and the suspect was eventually cleared of any involvement. Both cases remain unsolved to this day."

"What did the attorney say when he heard Grant Woods's story?" Jonas pressed.

"He thought the boy had made it all up to get back at his daughter, because she was friends with the kid who'd beaten him up at school."

Jonas considered what he'd just learned, recalling Emily's story about Grant and the girl he'd taken for a ride, then assaulted. If Grant was retaliating once again for that old wound, he certainly had a long memory. Although it wasn't impossible, it seemed highly unlikely.

"Many secrets have remained hidden over the years, but they're all coming to the surface now, so watch yourself," Diné Nééz said.

"I intend to," he answered.

"Have you been able to find any sign of Dinétsoh?"

"I know he passed through her land. I think he could be hiding in one of the old mines," Jonas said, updating him.

"Our searchers didn't find tracks around any of those openings. Don't go into those death traps unless you have hard evidence that the others missed. Judging from the amount of blood you found, Dinétsoh was fighting for his life, and may have already lost that battle," Diné Nééz said.

"Even if he did, the bearer bonds are still out there—maybe buried, or hidden under a rock. I'll keep searching, but there's a lot of ground to cover."

"We'll continue our search, too, but you've already found far more than any of the others."

"I believe he's up there somewhere," Jonas said again, pursing his lips and pointing toward the cliffs to the south.

Diné Nééz reached into his jacket and brought out a small leather pouch. "This *jish* was made for you," he said, handing it to him. "It has soil from the sacred mountains, pollen and other substances. It also contains something special that may prove of value to you—*shashchiin,* bear fetishes. One made out of turquoise and the other, jet. They are the guardians of boundaries. They'll provide you with protection."

"*Ahéhee',*" he replied, thanking him.

"It was Bear who helped the Diné defeat our enemies and enabled the People to live outside the shadow of fear," Diné

Nééz said. "Mother Earth is filled with power and offers her protection to those who honor her with prayers."

"Although a part of me still believes in the old ways, I prefer to rely on my own training when facing a challenge, Uncle," Jonas said.

"The two can work together, and make you even stronger."

Diné Nééz stood as Jonas fastened the bundle to his belt.

"I have reason to believe that the woman I'm guarding is protecting a secret of her own," Jonas said.

"One that pertains to the matter at hand?" he asked quickly.

"I don't know."

"If I learn anything that might be helpful, I'll call you right away."

Jonas left a short time later and was soon on the road back to Emily's place. As he reached the spot he'd chosen to stay at tonight—he changed positions nightly—Jonas greeted the sentinel who'd taken his place.

"Everything's quiet," his fellow warrior said. "The trailer curtains are mostly drawn, but if you take a look through the crack, you can see that she's got one small light, possibly a night-light, still on."

"Not a bad idea," Jonas said softly. "Evil is always friends with the dark."

Chapter Eleven

On Wednesday, Emily woke up right after sunrise. She looked outside, pleased with the progress Ken and his men had made. Yesterday, the work crew had come in early, finished leveling the site, and had actually managed to get the wood forms ready and the ground plumbing in and tested.

She'd received many calls about the furniture and other items she'd listed for sale, so while she'd handled that, Jonas had spent the day searching for Dinétsoh.

After twenty-four hours of relative peace, eight hundred dollars in her purse and her inn showing signs of progress, she felt more confident than she had in days.

Shortly after eight, Jonas came to her trailer. She smiled as his gaze slid over her appreciatively. "Come in," she invited. As he took a seat, she brought out some papers. "Last night I used my wireless to access Robert Jefferson's Web site. I printed out his photo and figure we can show it around. Maybe someone in town will remember seeing him recently."

"Good thinking."

"While surfing the net I also found a photo of Grant. I thought we could take that with us to the county records office this morning. The contract had the signature of the county clerk, so let's see if she remembers him."

They were in his truck and on their way to town a few minutes later.

"What's your biggest worry right now?" Jonas asked, hoping to surprise her into giving him a quick, truthful answer. When she hesitated, he knew that although he'd get a response, it wouldn't be *the* answer—the secret she was keeping from him.

"Despite the money I raised yesterday, my biggest worry is still funding," she said at last.

"You want this badly enough to find a way around obstacles. You'll make things work."

Emily gave him a surprised look. "Sounds like you have more faith in me than I do."

"I've spent the past few years around people who are trained to do the impossible. From what I've seen of you so far, you'd fit right in with them."

"Thanks," she said. "The inn means the world to me. It's something solid—my future. And it's all I've got left."

"Not *all*. You still have friends." He took her hand in his. Permanence and stability—what she seemed to want most—were two qualities he would never be able to provide for her. But what he could do was help her achieve her goal.

"No matter what happens, I'm not going to give up. I have this fire inside me that pushes me to keep going—to do whatever it takes to get my inn up and running."

That inner fire warmed him, as well, because it was rooted in hope, a quality he'd sacrificed a long time ago to training and resolve.

It took about forty minutes to reach the county government complex, a large, modern, two-story building located in the small city of Aztec. After a short walk through the parking lot, they reached the records office, located at the end of a long hall.

They went up to the counter, and a small, middle-aged woman who'd been seated behind one of the desks came up to meet them.

"May I help you?" she asked, pushing back a strand of gray-white hair. Her name tag identified her as Alice Sanchez.

Emily showed her a copy of the signed drilling-rights contract. "We have reason to believe that some of these signatures were forged. What we'd like you to do is tell us if your signature is genuine."

Mrs. Sanchez looked at the contract, then shook her head. "If I'd signed that, it would have had the notary seal right next to my name, and that's not there." She put on reading glasses, then studied the place where her name appeared. "That's also not even close to my handwriting. I bring the loop of my *S* all the way around, tucking it to the right of the letter. This one has a loop that's open and ends on the left side."

"Was this contract ever officially filed with the county?" Emily asked.

"It has a document number, so let me check the record files for you." Mrs. Sanchez entered the number on a keyboard, then double-checked the screen and the document. "This file number brings up a property deed listing for a house in Bloomfield, miles from your address—obviously the wrong document. But let me cross-check with your address and see if anything comes up. The numbers may have been entered incorrectly."

A few seconds later, she looked up. "Nothing." She stood. "Let's go talk in one of the conference rooms. We can speak privately there."

Signaling to another employee, she led the way down a long hallway. Once they were inside the small room, she invited them to take a seat at the circular table.

"This is very disturbing to me. We've never had any scandal here in my department," Mrs. Sanchez said. "And now a forgery of my own signature, no less!" She shook her head. "I'll have to report this to my boss."

"Do you know who might have the skill to create a credible document like this one?" Jonas asked.

She hesitated, then, as if making up her mind, admitted, "Several months ago, when we moved into this new office, the department hired a temporary employee by the name of Phil Davis. I came back from vacation a few days ago and found out that Mr. Davis had been terminated for improper conduct and 'irregularities.' When I tried to get specifics, I ran into a stone wall with my boss. No one would tell me anything. I was told to drop the matter and hire someone else."

"Unofficially, do you have any idea what happened?" Jonas pressed.

"Now that I see this, I'm thinking he was falsifying contracts and forging signatures. Phil liked taking shortcuts."

"What kind of shortcuts?" Jonas asked.

"Not bothering to file important paperwork when he was pressed for time, not logging in calls or updating records and generally letting things slide until the next day if it was close to quitting time," she said. "But you didn't hear that from me, okay?"

"No problem." Emily reached into her purse. "Do you recognize either of these men?"

"I know both. Mr. Woods there," she said, pointing, "is a private accountant who takes on work for the county on occasion. The other is Robert Jefferson. He's a real-estate attorney who's involved in many of the property transactions that come through this office. I've never had any problems with either of them."

Jonas and Emily thanked Mrs. Sanchez, then left the office. While inside the building, neither said a word, but once they reached the parking lot, Emily was the first to speak.

"The fact that both Grant and Robert are seen as solid citizens is going to make things tougher for us. Word's bound to reach them. Public employees usually prefer to stay on the good side of anyone with a lot of money and power."

"It's worth pushing for answers, anyway," Jonas said. "But you're right. The wealthy always have more leeway."

"Grant's involvement in this still doesn't make sense to me. He might *want* my land, but he doesn't *need* it."

"Sometimes wanting is enough."

"If that's the case, maybe he figured out that this phony agreement—even if I can eventually prove it's invalid—is a good way to sabotage, or at least delay my sale to the tribe. And, of course, if I go broke in the meantime and *have* to sell, so much the better. He'll be right there, hoping to snap up my property at bargain-basement prices."

"We need to stir things up and see what comes to the surface," Jonas said.

"I hate looking for trouble, but in this case, I think you're right. I want to know who my enemy is. I'm tired of fighting shadows."

He smiled in approval. Emily was his type of woman. "Keep in mind there's a slim chance that Grant Woods doesn't know the contract's phony. It's possible he was victimized, too. He might have counted on the integrity of another party he authorized to cut a deal with your father. Without talking to Grant, which we can't do without tipping our hand, we won't know for sure who drew up that contract for him, and if he just assumed the signatures were legit. If he believes your father initiated the deal, that would mean someone is conning him, as well."

"Like maybe Robert Jefferson, who has now conveniently disappeared?" she answered.

"That's one possibility. What we need to do is follow the money, and that'll take us to Phil Davis next. Let's see what I can do to find him."

"Your sources will help," she said with a nod.

It hadn't been a question, more like an acknowledgment. Remembering how she'd linked the circle and the flames to the tribe, he considered the possibility that she knew about the Brotherhood. Her father had known, and although Powell Atkins had sworn to keep the secret, it was possible Emily had seen or overheard something over the years. It would explain her comment. Then again, the Brotherhood's insignia had been on the contract that had cited a shadow tribal agency—their cover.

He was overanalyzing things. That was all. The fact was only a few knew about the Brotherhood.

"What if we never find the answers we need?"

"We will," he stated firmly. "Believe me."

"I do," she said, then sighed softly. "You've never lied to me, even back then…" She shook her head, almost as if regretting the words, and lapsed into silence.

Her whisper had felt like a tender caress, soothing his scarred heart. "That night will be a part of both of us forever." He started to reach again for her hand, but stopped himself.

He was a warrior. That's all he'd ever been and all he would ever be. He didn't want, or need, a family who counted on him.

To pull a soul as gentle as hers into the kind of life he led would be wrong. She deserved better.

Using one hand, he flipped open his cell phone, then cursed under his breath. "No signal. I'm going to pull over and see if I have better luck outside. I'll be back in a minute, hopefully with a lead on Davis."

Chapter Twelve

Emily watched him move away. Everything about Jonas sang to her, touching her in ways that left her feeling vulnerable and wonderfully feminine all at the same time. Love, though the gentlest of all emotions, was the most difficult to deny.

He returned to the truck moments later, and slipped behind the wheel. "I'm going to drop you off at home—well, your trailer. There's some business I need to handle alone."

Her eyes narrowed. "You know where Davis is, don't you?"

He nodded. "I thought I'd follow him and see where that takes me. But things can get ugly fast in situations like this."

"I'm going with you," she said flatly.

Jonas shook his head. "It's too dangerous."

"You're not locking me out of this. This is *my* fight, and I'm in it to the end."

Her words resonated with conviction, and he knew he'd never talk her out of it. "You're one hell of a woman," he murmured, then brushed her cheek with his knuckles. Pure masculine pride filled him as he felt her shiver in response. She had the courage of a dozen warriors, but she was all woman. He needed her—

The thought brought his musings to a crashing halt.

"We better get going. We've got a lot of work to do."

Although she'd sensed Jonas's abrupt change in mood,

she wasn't sure what had caused it. As she looked over, all she could see in his face was self-control and steely determination.

Maybe that's what he needed from himself right now to fight the evil that was pressing in on them. She'd have her own battle to wage soon enough—not only against flesh and blood, but against the darkness that was closing in on her.

"Davis is supposed to be at his new job," he said, interrupting her thoughts. "He works behind the counter at a gas station out on east Main. Let's stake out the location and see if any of his friends drop by. When we're ready, we'll make our move."

"Sounds good to me." Emily wasn't sure what kind of move he wanted to make, but she was ready to do whatever it took to get answers.

They arrived at the gas station ten minutes later. Jonas parked on a side street, facing the station. "We'll have a good view from here, since the cash register is right next to the window."

"Is that him?" she asked, seeing a man with bulging biceps going to the counter and ringing up a purchase for an elderly woman.

"Yeah." Jonas nodded, flipped his phone open, then showed her the photo he'd been sent. "Add a few years to this picture and you get the guy by the window."

"He looks like he's been working out a lot since that was taken. His biceps are the size of my waist."

"He's been in prison. A lot of the inmates pump iron to fight the boredom. They also pick up criminal skills—like forgery, apparently, in his case."

"How do you think he ended up working for the county?"

"The mayor's policy is to give cons a second chance. Looks like good ol' Phil got his chance, then blew it. If he's on parole, he's lucky not to be back in prison."

After watching for about a half hour, they saw Phil arguing with someone in the garage bay, a person not visible from their angle. A few minutes later, Phil stormed out of the office and jumped into an old gray sedan.

"We're going to follow him from a distance," Jonas said, starting the engine. Pulling out into traffic, they proceeded west into the city. Making a left turn, they entered an old, run-down neighborhood known for its high crime level and gang activity. Jonas glanced over at Emily. "Keep your door locked and don't make eye contact with *anyone*."

Seeing a group of boys gathered in front of a bar, she did as he asked. Yet, instead of following his own advice and avoiding eye contact, Jonas met their stares with an unflinching one of his own, followed by a somber nod.

"Are you trying to provoke them?"

"Just the opposite. To a Navajo, avoiding eye contact is a sign of respect but out here it's different. If *I* looked away, those kids would perceive it as a sign of weakness and, like predatory animals, they're more prone to attack then. The nod acknowledges their presence, and makes them think we've met before."

His voice was cold and detached, edged with steely resolve. Jonas was in full warrior mode now, and that left no room for the gentle man who'd loved her so tenderly.

She braced herself, determined to also become whatever she needed to be in order to face what lay ahead. She wasn't a soldier, just a woman fighting to build a dream—but there was no fiercer warrior than one whose heart was committed to the fight.

"Where do you think Phil's going?" she asked, her voice steady.

"My guess is he's heading to a residential section south of the river. Most of the houses there are rentals, and in pretty bad shape. The whole area reeks of garbage, since the people living there have quit caring. But they have to. Otherwise life'll destroy them one inch at a time."

She wondered if that's how it had been for him—hardened by war and poverty here at home. Did he think that if he allowed himself to care too much—even about her—it would somehow destroy him? Yet the ability to care was what made them human, and lifted them above the debris life too often left behind.

"There he goes," Jonas said abruptly.

Phil climbed out of his car, and as they passed by, she watched him enter a small house with a torn screen door hanging off one hinge. The minimal wood trim on the building needed fresh paint, and the walls were covered with a scratch coat of gray stucco. Dried weeds from last summer choked the yard, and the mailbox was missing from its wooden post. Nothing about those four walls and roof evoked the concept of home.

Once they reached the end of the block, Jonas turned around and drove back down the street. "I'm going to have a talk with Mr. Davis. You might want to keep the doors locked, and wait here in the truck."

"I'm going in with you. If there's trouble, I'll be there to help."

His eyebrows rose, and the hint of a smile touched the corners of his mouth. "What exactly would you do—theoretically?"

"I can't fight, but what made me a good resort manager, and will make me a great innkeeper, is my ability to communicate with people. Reason and persuasion can work wonders. I might be able to keep things from getting out of hand."

He shook his head slowly and let his breath out in a hiss. "If you insist on coming along, then make sure you stay a couple of steps behind me."

As they walked to the front door, she could feel Jonas's tension. He was as taut as a bowstring. His eyes darted everywhere, and he seemed attuned to everything around them.

Standing to one side of the door, he knocked hard, watching the window curtain for activity.

As her eyesight continued to fade, Emily's sense of hearing had grown acute—or at least more focused. When Jonas knocked for a second time, she heard the very faint sound of footsteps around the corner of the house. Placing her hand on Jonas's arm, she cocked her head to the right.

Jonas edged away and, with a nod, motioned for her to keep knocking. Just as Emily knocked again, he reached around the corner and yanked Davis forward by his shirt collar.

His quarry exploded, punching him in the chest and breaking loose. Jonas kicked out and caught the big man in the gut, slamming him into the wall so hard the window beside him cracked.

Davis came rushing back, tackling Jonas on the driveway. As they went down, Jonas kneed his attacker in the groin, rolled and came up on his feet.

The other man was almost as quick, leaping from the ground to a low crouch in an instant. He lunged for his car door, yanking it open as a barrier between them.

Jonas punched through the open window, catching Davis in the upper chest. He kicked the door next, hoping to pin him, but the other man slipped free, throwing a counter punch that missed Jonas's jaw by an inch.

Emily edged closer, looking around for a weapon and trying to figure out how best to help. Both men were remarkably agile and in good shape, though Jonas, less bulky, was quicker on his feet. So far they'd blocked each other's blows, but that couldn't last. Eventually one of them would score a major hit.

As Jonas blocked another blow with his forearm, she spoke quickly. "Phil, I'm the only one who can keep you out of prison, so stop fighting and start listening. I've got proof that you forged the drilling-rights contract," she bluffed, with all the confidence she could muster. "But I'm not after you. I want Grant Woods, or whoever hired you for the job. Tell me who that is, and we'll walk away."

"And that's it? No cops?" Davis asked, rubbing his jaw as he circled Jonas slowly.

Jonas stood his ground, his eyes never leaving his opponent.

Emily stepped back, staying out of Phil's range. "That's it. I get the information I need, and we walk away. No cops. It's a fair trade," she said, praying he'd fall for her bluff. The truth was she had no proof of anything.

Almost as if he'd had the same thought, his eyes narrowed. "What kind of proof do you have against me?"

"Your work has certain…shall we say trademarks?" Jonas answered for her. "If we take what we've got to the law, or the parole board—you'll be back in Santa Fe before the weekend."

"But you're not our target," Emily repeated. "We don't want to waste our time on the hired help—we want the boss. Cooperate and we're gone."

Davis brushed away a trickle of blood from the corner of his mouth with his sleeve. "Yeah, yeah. We can work something out. Let's go inside, I'm feeling a little thirsty."

The living room-kitchen was clean and smelled of fresh paint. A small TV stood in a corner. There was a torn sofa and a wooden kitchen table with three chairs. "Beer?" Phil asked, walking over and opening the fridge.

"Just information," she answered, after glancing at Jonas and seeing him shake his head. "But thanks for offering."

"No prob," Davis replied, opening his beer with a whoosh and taking a deep swallow. "I did forge the contract you're talking about," he said, holding the cold bottle against his jaw. "I learned that trade in the pen. It was some of my best work, too, though I couldn't get to the clerk's notary stamp. That would have sealed the deal, literally. But don't think I'm holding out on you when you hear the rest. I can't tell you who hired me, not for sure."

"Can't or won't?" Jonas countered.

"Can't," Davis answered. "No games, man. All I know about Grant Woods is that his was the only signature I wasn't asked to forge. I was paid by a blonde, who turned out to be using a phony name. I should have guessed that, considering the job, but I only found out when I tried to track her down. She sure wasn't phony where it counted—hot bod, low-cut top, skintight shorts. You should have seen her."

"How did she contact you?" Jonas pressed.

"She just showed up here about a week ago. She gave me a copy of the text, samples of the signatures she wanted forged, and two days to get the job done. She came back right on schedule, dressed and looking the same as the first time—hot, hot, hot. She checked the job, paid me in cash and that's the last I saw of her. Wish I'd have gotten a look at her plates. Maybe I could have tracked her down."

"And you have no idea who she was?"

"None. I asked around plenty, too. She's not the kind any man's likely to forget, but I didn't get anywhere."

"Give me a better description of her," Jonas said.

"Midtwenties, five-two, bottle blonde but who cares, dark eyes, nice smile and, man, was she *built*."

"That description could fit a number of women. Anything specific?" Jonas said.

"I never looked past her…top," he admitted, giving Emily a sheepish look. "There was more than enough there to hold my attention, if you know what I mean." He paused. "Come to think of it, she played it real smart, focusing my attention like that. There was nothing, except her clothes and those…to ID her. No jewelry, watch or anything."

Emily remained quiet until Jonas and she were back in the truck, heading out of the neighborhood. "That woman must be connected to either Grant or Robert Jefferson."

"If you think about what Davis said, ignoring the clothes— and the hair, which sounded like a wig to me—the description could fit Jefferson's legal assistant."

"Jen?" She remembered the woman in the sensible business suit. "She's good-looking enough, and certainly has the figure. But it's hard to imagine her in the kind of outfit Davis described."

"Exactly. That's why she wore it. Most men would have had their eyes fixed on her—" he stopped abruptly, then added "—her other attributes, not her face."

"If it really was Jen, then it seems likely she was working with Jefferson. If I recall correctly, she didn't like Grant, because he'd hit on her."

"That could have been an act meant to misdirect us. We can't rule out the possibility that maybe Woods paid her to do the job," Jonas mused.

"So we're still nowhere. We can't prove a thing."

"The Navajo Way teaches that everything is connected. Nothing happens without affecting something else. Once we identify the overall pattern that weaves the events together, we'll be able to restore balance."

Emily gazed at him for a long moment. "The Navajo perspective brings beauty and practicality. You can't beat that."

"My number one priority is always to restore harmony." He glanced at his bruised knuckles and gave her one of his devastatingly masculine grins. "But to do that it's sometimes necessary to get a little dirty."

"You enjoyed that fight!"

"Enjoyed?" His eyes held an almost dangerous gleam. "I wouldn't say that. But I do whatever has to be done. That means I can be nothing but trouble for some people."

The edge in his voice caught her attention, and she suddenly realized that he was warning her. "Life comes with trouble. It's one way of keeping us alert and helping us take notice of the good things we already have," she replied.

Jonas felt the gentle strength behind her words. Her sense of mission made her an unstoppable force. Even if he hadn't been under orders, he would have stood beside her. Though their ways of fighting were vastly different, she was a warrior in her own right—one who'd claimed a piece of his heart.

Chapter Thirteen

As they headed back to her home, awareness shimmered between them. Being with Jonas was exciting, Emily mused, though admittedly, a little boredom every once in a while would have been fine with her, too.

As they approached the work site, the lack of activity got her attention instantly. "Where's the rest of the crew, and the cement mixer?" From what she could see, there were only three men present, and they were just standing around. The wooden forms for the concrete foundation were in place along with rebar, and the ground work on the plumbing had been finished, but no work was under way. "I was told they'd be busy pouring the new foundation today."

As Jonas parked, Ken jogged over to meet them. "I've got some bad news. I've had to postpone the concrete delivery until noon because I'm having trouble getting a full work crew here this morning. Several of my men had their vehicles vandalized last night—everything from a smashed windshield to slashed tires. And there was another surprise waiting here for the ones who made it in. Someone drew weird figures on the side of the portable shed where we keep our supplies. The tribal guys took off after one of my framers said they looked like Navajo witchcraft symbols drawn with corpse poison."

"Where did you say the drawings were?" Jonas asked, getting out of his pickup.

Ken gestured ahead.

Jonas walked over to the shed and studied what appeared to be a charcoal drawing of a snake with an odd diamond pattern on its back. Beside it was a horned stick figure. "I don't know what this is, but it's not Navajo witchcraft. Someone took Navajo lore and Christian symbols of evil, and mixed them together. The horned guy, I'm thinking, is the devil. The snake thrown into the mix is supposed to represent evil, I guess, but in Navajo tradition, Snake isn't evil. Snake represents the Lightning People, who bring us rain."

"What about that corpse poison stuff?" Ken asked.

Jonas took a look at the powdery substance and sniffed it. "It's charcoal—corpse poison is made of other ingredients you don't want to hear about. This is just an attempt to scare people. Who said it was corpse poison?"

"Larry Green. He's married to a Navajo woman."

"Is he still here?" Jonas asked.

"Yeah, right over there," Ken said, pointing.

"Let's go talk to him," Jonas said.

As they walked down the road toward the group of workers, Jonas saw one man turn and walk casually toward the parked vehicles, not making eye contact.

"Is that Green?" Jonas asked, moving to cut him off.

"Yeah," Ken answered.

Seeing Jonas had blocked him from his truck, Green sprinted into the *bosque*. Jonas took off after him. He was used to running for miles at a grueling pace in heavy combat boots, often with full gear. He knew he could outdistance Green easily, even though the man had a good head start.

When it became clear that Green was circling, intending on returning to his truck, Jonas increased his speed, running like the wind.

He was closing in when Green suddenly stopped, whirled around and dived at his knees. Jonas dodged the tackle with a fake to the right, and Green fell headfirst into the dirt. As Jonas turned to move in, his opponent flipped onto his back and kicked out, narrowly missing his groin.

Green scrambled to his feet, but Jonas delivered a hard punch to his solar plexus in the process. Green reeled and fell into the brush behind him, gasping for air.

Jonas cut him off just in case he tried to make one final attempt to reach the truck. "Move and I'll put some holes in your ride," he said, opening his jacket enough to show the Beretta at his side. "Those tires look new. I'll start with them."

"Don't do that. I'm done running," the man muttered, sitting on the ground.

Ken and Emily ran up just then.

"Larry, what the heck are you up to, man?" Ken demanded angrily. "Did you draw that crap on the shed?"

"It was him, all right," Jonas said, before he could answer. "Look at his hands. He's still got charcoal under his fingernails. Call the sheriff and let the deputies sort this out."

"Deputies?" Larry got up slowly, putting his arms out, palms up, as Jonas took a step toward him. "Ease up, man. So I drew some stuff on a wall. You've got me for graffiti, or tagging or whatever you call it. But it'll wash off. So what's the big deal?"

"You scared off some of my men," Ken yelled. "What the heck were you thinking? We don't do the work, *nobody* gets paid."

"It's just a prank, boss. Take a pressure washer to it and it'll come right off," he said. "There was no real harm done. These days we can all use a few extra bucks."

"Is that why you did this? Extra bucks?" Jonas pressed.

"Yeah. And again, what's the harm? So some guys got spooked. It was that stuff I said about corpse poison that really got them worried," he added, laughing.

"Do you know what corpse poison is?" Jonas snapped.

"It's supposed to be ground-up bones—like the stuff Navajo witches collect. I knew about that because of my wife. When she found out my will specified that I be cremated and my ashes scattered, she went a little nuts. She said that was corpse poison and she wouldn't touch it."

"Did you screw with J.D.'s and Billy's pickups, too?" Ken demanded. "If you did, I've got news for you, buddy. They're going to take it out of your hide."

"That wasn't me, boss. I wouldn't mess with anyone's truck," he added quickly.

"If you're lying and the law finds your fingerprints on those trashed vehicles, or a witness points you out, forget about apologies and excuses. Either pay up on the spot when the guys get here, or they're going to take it out on that shiny pickup of yours."

"I didn't do anything to their stuff," he protested. "No way I'd ever mess with someone's ride."

"Save yourself some major-league trouble. Tell me who hired you to put up that graffiti. Were you told what to draw?" Jonas pressed.

"A girl—well, a woman—approached me. I don't know her name. She told me it had to look like witchcraft, the Navajo kind, and to make it scary. She figured I'd be able to get the information I'd need from my wife, but Clara never talks about stuff like that. She says it calls evil to you."

"So where did you get the idea for those drawings, and what are they supposed to mean?" Emily asked, glancing back at the shed.

"The stick figure with the horns, that's like the devil, you know? And everyone's afraid of snakes, right? I put some extra lines on the body because I thought that would make it look more like a rattler."

Jonas glared at him. "The woman who hired you—tell me more about her. Start with what she looked like."

"I never saw her. She was just a voice over my cell phone. But she knew my name and told me what she wanted. I asked to meet her. She had a real sexy voice and I was just curious, you know? But she said no, and told me that I either did things her way or not at all. The morning after I agreed to do the job for her, I found an envelope in my truck, and a typed note saying I'd get the other half after the job was done."

"Where's the note?" Jonas demanded.

"I threw it out. But, hey, she still owes me the second half. Why don't you stake out my truck? Maybe she'll come by to-night. It's worth a shot, right?"

Jonas stared at him in disbelief. "Einstein, do you really think you're going to get paid now? She got what she wanted."

"And, Larry, you're fired," Ken added. "Grab your tools and get out of here."

"Hey, come on! Just for a little graffiti? Give me a break."

"You cost me an entire morning's work."

Emily saw the expression of sheer dismay on Green's face and felt a wave of sympathy. "Ken, give him one more chance. He really had no idea what he was doing."

"I didn't think it was such a big deal. Really," Green insisted.

"You've got a good heart, Emily," Ken said, then glanced at Larry. "I don't want to look at your dumb face, so forget about getting paid for today. Come back tomorrow and see if you've still got a job."

"Yeah, fine," Larry muttered. As they watched, he climbed into his truck and drove off.

Ken rubbed the back of his neck with one hand. "This job's been full of surprises. And after such a good day yesterday, I thought we were finally on track." As he gazed toward the work site, one of the other men whistled, then motioned for him to come over.

"Now what?" Ken grumbled.

"Maybe something else was tampered with," Emily said,

noting that the worker was standing in the area where the biggest cluster of pipes had been installed.

"Don't tell me Larry messed up the ground plumbing," Ken muttered. "We've already pressure tested everything, and it was ready for the foundation to be poured."

The three of them walked across the metal rebar toward the collection of pipes protruding from the ground.

Pipes…the beginning of her dream. Emily had just formed a picture of the finished inn in her mind when she heard her foreman curse.

"Somebody's drilled holes in half the supply and drain pipes just above ground level. We're going to have to repair or replace the entire system now." He looked at Emily, shaking his head. "There's no way we can pour the foundation today."

"Was it Larry's doing?" Emily asked, trying to make some sense out of it all. "As I recall, he was the first one here. And he was alone when we left for town. That was probably when he put up those drawings."

Ken spat out an oath, his face red. "Larry! If I find out he was responsible for this, too, I'm going to hang him up to dry." He reached for his cell phone. "I'm going to cancel the concrete and send the sheriff over to his place right now."

"Do you really think he'd do this? He would have been cutting his own throat—putting himself out of a day's work or more for sure," Jonas said.

"Yeah, you're right about that," Ken said reluctantly. "Larry comes across as rock-stupid sometimes, but he works hard and is always looking for overtime." The foreman rubbed the back of his neck yet again. "This isn't just a malicious prank. This is destruction of property. It goes beyond the kind of thing Larry would pull. But prank or not, Larry's done some serious harm, too. That corpse-poison stuff really spooked some of my men. If they refuse to come back, I'm going to have to look for replacements, and that'll take time."

"Getting the facts from another Navajo should straighten things out quickly," Jonas said. "Give me their addresses and I'll go talk to your men."

"That's a great plan. They'll listen to one of their own," Ken said. "Just keep in mind that the ones who've had their pickups vandalized aren't going to be in a good mood. Add the fact that they don't know you, other than having seen you around… You get my meaning?"

"It'll work out. Trust me," Jonas said.

"Okay. I'll get you the addresses." He turned and walked off toward his pickup.

As soon as Ken was out of earshot, Jonas turned to Emily. "You should consider staying here. I'm not sure what kind of reception I'll get."

"I can handle myself and do whatever the situation calls for. Stop trying to keep me on the sidelines," she said, anger in her voice.

She looked beautiful, filled with fire, and more than a match for him. He smiled and threw up his hands. "I give up. It's your call."

Ken arrived with the addresses before she could say anything else. "Here they are. You might also tell the men that I said for them to get their butts in gear if they want to keep their jobs."

JONAS AND EMILY WERE on the road soon after, heading toward the west side of the city across the river. "The first address isn't far," he said, "just south of the hospital. Once we're there, stay alert to subtle body language. That'll telegraph trouble before it happens."

"Don't worry about me. Focus on what you have to do," she said, tilting her head to get a clearer look at the road ahead.

Today the vision in her right eye was particularly dim. It was like trying to see through a sheet of wax paper. She'd hoped the condition would straighten out as the day went by, but it wasn't any better.

As the world around her faded from view, the feeling of isolation that seemed to dog her footsteps these days tightened its grip. Refusing to dwell on things she couldn't change, she tried to think positive. At least the vision in her left eye continued to hold steady.

"Is your eyesight giving you problems again?" Jonas asked.

"It's probably just stress. The pressure's really mounting on all fronts lately," she said, deflecting his question. She didn't want to lie, but wasn't ready to share this part of her life with him.

"I'm guessing it's far more than that," he said gently.

"Don't ask me for answers I can't give you."

"Can't or won't?"

She didn't respond right away. As much as she wanted someone to talk to, to share her fears with, those kinds of revelations stripped the soul bare. Once she did that, there'd be no turning back. To deepen the connection between them, to add a spiritual intimacy, seemed foolhardy. She needed to keep a strong wall between them—a barrier he couldn't cross. That separation would allow her to cultivate her own strength so she could face whatever lay ahead.

"I haven't asked you about the secrets you keep—and you do have them," she said at last. "Respect my privacy and stop pushing me for more than I can give you." The ache of loneliness touched her heart, but she brushed the feeling aside firmly, knowing her path was set.

"You're a strong woman, Emily, but don't shut me out. If you let me, maybe I can help," he said.

"You *are* helping me. The Tamarisk Inn means more to me than you realize. It's going to be a place where people with special needs won't have to feel isolated. They'll be able to go anywhere safely. The key word will be *accessibility*. My inn will be a place of freedom, and it'll become known for strengthening its guests from the inside out." She paused for a moment, trying to find the right words. "My dream and who I am…are one and the same."

Jonas nodded, understanding far more than her words had revealed. Emily was all about hope, about beating the odds. And she'd brought a new gentleness into his life, a quality he'd never thought would warm his days and nights again.

He focused on the road, and swore under his breath. He had to get it through his thick skull that Emily was *off-limits.* But even as the thought formed, he knew that he'd never stop wanting her. Though he'd eventually have to leave, Emily would haunt his dreams for the rest of his life.

FIFTEEN MINUTES LATER, JONAS pulled up behind a police car parked on a narrow street. The driveway directly ahead held a new-looking truck with a smashed windshield. The hood of the pickup was covered with a gray, powdery substance.

A Navajo police officer was speaking to another man, apparently the owner of the truck. Emily recognized him as a member of Ken's crew.

As the officer came out of the open garage, he glanced at Jonas and gave him a nod. Something about the look the men exchanged assured Emily that they knew each other. That was confirmed a short time later when he approached them.

"That's one angry Navajo," the officer said, his voice low. "If he catches the man who messed up his truck, it'll take a K-9 to get him off."

Jonas glanced at the truck owner, who was using a hand broom and dustpan to brush the gray powder off of his truck. "Ashes?" Jonas asked.

"Yeah, but take a good look at the color. Though the perp was probably hoping they'd be mistaken for human ashes, my guess is they came from someone's fireplace."

"The vic—did he think it was corpse poison?" Jonas asked.

"Nah, not after he heard from some of the others on his work crew. One guy who had his tires slashed was Apache, not Navajo. He decided to wipe off the ashes with a paper towel, and found a chunk of wood in the mix. It still had a roofing nail in it."

"This is just another attempt to slow down or sabotage construction at my place," Emily said.

"Are you finished here?" Jonas asked the officer, who was eyeing her with curiosity.

When he saw Jonas watching him, the deputy nodded, and tried unsuccessfully to hide a grin. "Yes, sir. All I can do is fill out a report. With the perpetual manpower shortage we have in the department, vandalism isn't at the top of our list of priorities."

"Okay, our turn," Jonas said to Emily. "Let's you and I go talk to the truck owner and see if we get anywhere."

The Navajo construction worker was sweeping up the glass with a push broom as Jonas and Emily approached. "I've already told you all I can, detectives," he said, not looking up.

"We're not the police," Jonas told him.

The man glanced up at Emily. "You're the property owner." Then he looked at Jonas. "I remember you from the site. But what are you two doing here?"

"We're checking into a related matter. Is there any opposition that you know about to Ms. Atkins's inn, or to the company hired to do the work?"

"If anyone has a complaint, it's no one from our crew. With the economy like it is, construction jobs are few and far between. We're all grateful to be employed. Are you thinking that whoever tried to vandalize the lumber is responsible for what happened to my truck?" He looked back at his pickup. "That puppy's brand-new, and now look at it! If I catch the guy who took out my windshield I'm going to feed him this glass."

"Have you seen anyone either at the site or around this neighborhood just hanging around?" Jonas asked.

He shook his head. "Ken told us to keep a lookout for problems. He told us about that vandalism a few days ago at the site. But, between the three of us, when I'm at work, I'm too busy to focus on anything else. The boss runs a tight ship. When I finally get home, it's usually late, and I'm tired. The kids on this street don't even mess with me."

Jonas and Emily left shortly thereafter. They were heading back out of town when a state police car came up beside them in the lefthand lane.

Jonas nodded to the officer, recognizing the Brotherhood warrior. The officer's car raced ahead, then pulled over to the side.

"Give me a moment," Jonas told Emily, slowing and parking behind the black-and-white unit.

From inside the cab, Emily watched Jonas meet the black-uniformed Indian officer who was standing between the two vehicles. She had a feeling that Jonas's Brotherhood connections were far more extensive than she'd originally thought.

As glad as she was for the extra help, she wondered if she'd ever find answers. Jonas believed that everything was connected, but only one constant tied all the events together. Dinétsoh's and Jefferson's disappearance, the vandalism and the phony contract all had one thing in common—her land. The place where she hoped to build her inn and face her future.

Chapter Fourteen

A moment later, Jonas returned. "I've got a lead on Robert Jefferson."

"Where is he?" she asked, sitting up.

"North of the state line, in the Durango area. He's staying at a motel called The Roadrunner. I understand it's strictly one star—maybe a half—but the place is supposed to be quiet and just outside the city limits. It'll take nearly two hours to get there and back, so I say we leave right now."

She took a deep breath, then nodded. "Yeah, let's go. Once we get there, let me be the one to confront him. If you lean on him, he'll just stall and drown you in excuses. I'm his client. I've got a better chance of getting answers from him on that basis alone. If need be, I can push him by threatening to expose him publicly. I may not have enough to get him charged, but his career would go down the drain if word of what he's done to me got out."

"That's not a bad strategy," Jonas said, mulling it over. "The trick will be not letting him know for sure how much evidence we have against him."

"Our showing up like this, unexpected, will hopefully throw him off. We'll use that to our advantage."

He gave an approving nod. Emily was smart and quick on the uptake. She'd get results. "We don't know what we'll find once we get to that motel, so stay on your guard. There's a lot at stake for everyone involved."

She remained quiet for some time, deep in her own thoughts. "I really envy you," she said at last.

"Me? Why?"

"Your heritage—it's a source of strength that never fails you."

"The Navajo Way sustains all the Diné. That's true enough. But you've found something else that gives you courage and keeps you going—the inn."

"My dream gives me focus, yes," she answered, measuring her words carefully.

He could sense what she'd left unsaid as clearly as if she'd shouted the words. As important as the inn was to her, she would need more in her life than just that.

The Navajo Way taught that to be complete, a man needed a woman's energy, and a woman needed a man's strength. As Jonas looked at her, he knew that Emily completed him in a way no one else ever could.

"I never knew that dreams could carry such a high price," she said softly. "But if I have to fight for mine, I can't think of anyone I'd rather have beside me."

The light in her eyes, and the feeling of her voice, wrapped themselves around him and tightened. The ever present knowledge that he'd eventually have to step out of her life felt like a bullet working its way to his heart.

LESS THAN AN HOUR later, they approached the southern outskirts of Durango. Off the right side of the highway was a false-fronted Old West–style building right out of a Hollywood movie, complete with wooden sidewalk and a hitching rail. The sign in the center of the facade above the office doors identified The Roadrunner Hotel.

"This must be the place. What's his room number, do you

know?" Emily asked as they pulled into the parking lot of the one-story motel.

Jonas told her, then parked in an empty space a few doors down from room 110. The curtains were drawn so it was impossible to see inside as they exited the vehicle.

"I'll go in first," he said, his voice all business.

He knocked loudly but no one answered. They could hear a radio playing country-and-western music, however.

"Someone's inside. He may not feel like answering, but we're staying put till he does." Jonas knocked again, even louder. "Jefferson, open up."

Emily waited, then on impulse tried the knob, and the door swung open. Jonas placed a hand on her shoulder, pulling her back, then stepped inside.

The first thing that hit him was the smell. It was one he knew well, a scent impossible to mistake for anything else. He glanced around the floor, searching for its source.

Emily, who was standing in the doorway, immediately clapped her hand to her mouth and nose. "What is *that?* It's horrible," she said, coughing, "like spoiled meat."

"You're close." The scent of death still filled his nightmares whenever he revisited scenes from his past in Iraq and Afghanistan. "Stay outside."

His warning came seconds too late. Emily had already entered the room, and as she stepped to the far side of the bed, she saw Jefferson's body on the carpeted floor. Her strangled cry blasted through Jonas. He went to her and, holding her close to his side, led her back out.

Emily melted against him, pressing her head to his heart. It was as if she desperately needed his warmth to reconnect with life and push back the specter of death.

Brushing his lips over her brow, he held her tightly for a moment, comforting her. "I have to go back in there," he said at last. He didn't want to let Emily go, but there was no choice. "Dial 911 while I go take a look around."

Duty drove him back into the room, and one quick glance at the body confirmed what he already knew. Robert Jefferson was long gone.

In the center of the attorney's greenish-red forehead was the entrance wound of a large-caliber bullet. His features were still recognizable, so that tended to indicate that the man had been dead for a day, max. In the Southwest, the heat invariably speeded up decomposition. Then again, it was comfortable inside the room, and the fact that the air-conditioning had kept the temperature in the low seventies would impact that time frame.

The medical investigator's office would have to narrow down the time of death, but Jefferson's check-in time would be recorded at the motel's desk, and that would help narrow the parameters.

Jonas took a quick look around, careful not to touch or step on anything. Blood splatter revealed that Jefferson had been shot and had fallen where he lay. There was no sign of a break-in, so that tended to indicate that he had known his killer, or at least hadn't felt threatened enough to bar him, or her, from entering.

Jonas went back outside and saw that Emily was still trembling. Her face had also grown several shades paler. Without any hesitation, he took her in his arms once more. "I'm sorry you had to see that."

She held on to him tightly. "I'll never forget what I saw in that room. Not ever," she whispered, remembering the soulless eyes staring at nothing…and the blood…so much blood.

The scent of death surrounded her still. It had seeped into her skin and clothes. More than ever she needed to reconnect with *life*.

Feeling the crush of Jonas's arms around her pushed back the blackness that threatened to overcome her. She nestled into him, needing more of his warmth. For this fragile moment in time, she would lean on him, and let love protect her.

TIME HAD PASSED WITH agonizing slowness and the Durango police seemed to be everywhere now. Emily remained standing next to Jonas's truck, waiting. The county M.E. had come and gone, and the body had been transported. As Emily waited for Jonas to join her, she listened to the bits and pieces of conversations going on around her.

Moments later, Jonas walked up to her. "His car's here and his wallet was untouched, but the police haven't found his BlackBerry," he said, avoiding mentioning the recently deceased by name.

"Do they have any idea who did this to him?" she asked, struggling to keep her voice steady.

"Not yet. The investigation's just begun."

"Any idea when he checked in? We saw him just two days ago, right?" she asked.

"Yeah, and according to the desk clerk, the attorney rented the room that same evening. There's no outside surveillance system, only in the office, so we don't know who came and left."

"So we may never find out now if he was connected to what's been happening around my place, or to Grant's forged contract," she said, trying to think of something other than what she'd seen in that room.

"I briefed the investigating officers on possible motives, so the detectives are going to get the paperwork needed to search his office and home. Although that'll require the cooperation of the Farmington police, it won't pose a problem," he said. "If the detectives find out that Jefferson had decided to blow the whistle on Grant and those forged papers, that'll turn Woods into their prime suspect. Of course, that'll depend on Woods's whereabouts at the time of the victim's death."

"Grant wants my land," she said. "But I don't think he's capable of doing this."

"Don't forget that he pulled a gun on me. And if he's as

wealthy as you say, he could have hired someone to do the job for him," Jonas pointed out.

"Like Sam, his handyman? Two men attacked me the night you came back into my life. Their faces were hidden, but their general descriptions fit Grant and Sam."

"Sam's one possibility, but without evidence, all we have is a theory. Keep in mind, too, that the dead man was an attorney. In that profession, success isn't measured just in the number of friends you make, but also in the number of enemies."

"Do you know if we're free to go?" she asked, seeing a tow truck hooking up Jefferson's vehicle.

"You've given them a statement, and so have I. We may have to speak to them again sometime down the line, but we can leave."

"Then let's get out of here. I want to put as much distance between us and this place as possible."

Jonas nodded, and they were on their way moments later. "You've seen some bad things today, Em, the kind that stick to a person," he said softly. "Don't try to handle those memories alone."

She wrapped her arms around herself and pressed back into the seat. "I'll be fine."

He glanced at her, then pulled off the road and parked. This time when he tried to take her into his arms, she resisted.

"I can't let you do this," she said. "I have to know that I can handle things on my own, even when life gets ugly."

"Human beings aren't wired that way, Em. We all have to reach out to someone else at one time or another."

"You don't," she said. "Emotionally, at least, you don't rely on anyone."

"You're wrong." He pulled her against him, and not giving her a chance to argue, smothered her protests with his mouth. He kissed her hungrily, in a way meant to make her forget everything but him, and as he did, heat filled him.

With a sigh, she surrendered to him, opening her mouth, giving him whatever he wanted to take. He was demanding and relentless, a fire that protected her from everything but itself. She gave in to it, greedily drinking in the pleasures he offered. This was *life*—the passion, the desire.

Soon the heat became too intense to control, and it was then that she reluctantly drew back. "You tempt me to throw caution to the wind, to forget everything but you. But I need more than moments."

The truth of her words cut through him like a knife. But, right or wrong, Jonas didn't want her to pull away. "What makes you so sure all I have to offer are moments?"

"Because you have your own destiny, and putting down roots isn't part of it."

He nodded slowly, then held her gaze. "I can't promise you forever, but I give you my word that before I go, you'll see your dream become a reality."

To *see* her dream… With all the delays in the construction and the problems with her finances, she wondered if that was even possible anymore. She took a steadying breath. That was one secret she couldn't share. It would kill her to see pity mirrored in his eyes.

Jonas started the engine and pulled back onto the highway. "I say we go pay Jen Caldwell another visit. If she's not at the office, we'll go visit her at home. I can find out where she lives."

Emily nodded, glad to get back to business. "That's a good idea. But how should we approach her?"

"With some straight talk. We'll tell Jen that her boss has been murdered, and see where that takes us."

"If you're hoping for the element of surprise, keep in mind that it's possible area detectives have already paid her a visit, and she knows what happened," Emily said.

"Surprise isn't as important as putting her on the defensive. We already suspect Jen arranged for the drilling-rights forgery, and very likely, Larry Green's handiwork at the construction site. It's also possible that she's a party to Jefferson's murder. We need to make her think we know more than we do and push her. Even if she's completely innocent, she might have information that's critical to the case—something she's keeping secret."

"That's entirely possible," Emily murmured softly. Secrets… Everyone had them. They thrived in the shadows because the light that could shatter their power often destroyed everything else in its path. And sometimes, in that darkness, they took on a life of their own.

Chapter Fifteen

They arrived at Robert Jefferson's office a little after five. The door was locked, but through the window they could see Jen standing inside, cell phone at her ear.

Emily knocked, and the woman jumped, obviously startled. When she realized who it was, she nodded and held up her hand.

At a glance, Emily could see that Jen had been crying, but it was the other emotion she saw etched on the woman's face that touched her most. She knew fear only too well—that feeling of helplessness in the face of danger, when everything inside you told you to run, but there was nowhere to go.

"Just a second," Jen called, folding up the phone and walking to the door. She let them in, stood back, then locked the door behind them quickly.

Emily's heart went out to her. "Are you okay?" she asked quietly.

Jen nodded, then in a broken voice added, "Mr. Jefferson... He's...gone. Murdered."

"We've heard."

"The police came by about fifteen minutes ago, but I didn't know what to tell them," she said, the words tumbling out. "They asked to take some of Mr. Jefferson's files, and I said yes, but now I'm wondering if I should have said no. The thing is, Mr. Jefferson's not married and has no close family. I didn't know who to ask."

"It's okay," Emily said. "You cooperated with the investigation, and that's the right thing to do. They're trying to find his killer."

Jen shuddered. "This whole thing is just so…crazy. Before the police left, they told me that I might be in danger. They don't know why Robert was killed—whether it had something to do with his business—and they're thinking that if it does, someone might come after me."

"Sit down and take a breath," Emily advised, trying to calm the woman.

Ignoring her, Jen continued pacing. "They said I should lock the doors and watch out for people who seemed to be hanging around. But I'm getting out of here," she said, her voice rising. "Since they told me not to leave town, I figured I'd go straight home. But what if someone's watching my place?"

"You're panicking, and that's the worst thing you can do," Jonas stated. "If the police felt you were in serious danger, they would have left someone outside. Just keep a clear head and you'll be fine."

Jen responded to Jonas's commanding tone instantly. It was the voice of a man who knew what he was talking about, and it inspired confidence. Emily sighed. Jonas was much too easy to rely on. That was part of the problem between them.

"Has Grant Woods come by the office since we last spoke?" she inquired, forcing her thoughts back to the present. As she spoke, she saw a flicker of alarm on Jen's face, but it was gone in an instant.

"No, he hasn't been here since last Friday, I think, when he came to visit Mr. Jefferson."

"Have you seen him passing by since, or parked along the curb, maybe?" Jonas asked, just to gauge her reaction.

"You mean, outside *this* office?" she repeated in alarm. "No, not at all. I told him I have a boyfriend—and besides,

I don't go out with clients who try to pick me up. Or any clients, actually."

Thinking of her own past, and all the conversations she'd overheard while on the job, Emily walked to the doorway that separated the reception area from Jefferson's office. "These walls aren't very thick. Have you ever heard Grant threaten your boss?"

"No. The police asked me the same thing about all our clients, wanting to know who Mr. Jefferson's enemies are…were. And that's why I'm getting out of here. You won't be the only ones who'll assume I know more than I do. If I don't lie low, I'll end up dead, too." She glanced at the clock on the wall, then back at them. "Is that it?"

"Yes," Jonas answered. "We'll be in touch."

As soon as they were outside, Jen locked the door behind them.

Jonas gestured for Emily to follow him, then led the way around the side of the building. His movements were completely silent. The landscaping gravel didn't even crunch under his feet. By comparison, she was as quiet as a herd of elephants.

The side of the old brick-and-stone building was lined with fragrant, neatly trimmed juniper bushes. Obeying his hand signal, she hung back as he looked through a side window of the office.

A moment later, he rejoined her. "I saw her get back on the phone. Although I couldn't hear much, I'm pretty good at reading lips. She's going to meet someone, so let's hang back, give her plenty of room, then follow."

"How did you learn to read lips?" Emily asked. It didn't sound like something he'd learned in the military.

"Necessity. I lost my hearing for about two months, and it was the only way I could follow what was going on," Jonas replied, his eyes on the road.

"What happened? Some childhood ear infection?" She tried to think what form of illness could cause something like that.

"No. More like two years ago. A suicide bomber got too close."

The expression on his face told her there was much more to the story. She started to ask, then stopped. They each had things they weren't willing to share. Knowing this was something Jonas didn't want to talk about, she allowed the matter to drop.

"You think Jen knows Grant a lot better than she's admitting?" she asked. "Maybe she wasn't as upset by his flirting as she wanted us to believe. Could he be the boyfriend she mentioned?"

"Jen's obviously terrified, and knows at least as much as we do about what's going on. We'll have to keep a close watch on her. Fear often makes people unpredictable."

"Do you think she knows who killed Jefferson?"

"Maybe not for certain, but my gut tells me that she knows who the most likely candidates are. It's that knowledge that makes her a threat to the killer," Jonas said.

They returned to his pickup, going around the rear of the building, through the alley so Jen wouldn't see them. While waiting for her to take off, Jonas made a quick call to someone he called Preston. Within seconds, they had Jen's address—an apartment on the northeast side of the city, several miles away.

Just as he was putting away his phone, the woman stepped outside the office, looked around nervously, then locked the door.

"She's coming this way," Jonas said quickly. "Duck down."

They heard footsteps on the sidewalk as she walked past, then the sound of her getting into a vehicle several spaces away. When it pulled out, they looked up and saw an SUV going west down Main Street. Jonas followed, staying well back, but being sure he made the stoplights in order to keep up.

"It doesn't look like she's heading home," Emily said quickly. "You think she's making a run for it?"

"No—at least not yet. My guess is that Jen's looking for help. In situations like these, people turn to those who mean the most to them. For her, it's probably her boyfriend. She could be going to his house."

"I wonder how carefully she's thought things through. Depending on who this guy is, she could be heading into even more danger."

He said nothing for several moments, intent on his driving. Once it was clear she was going to continue west out of town instead of turning north, he relaxed. "Right now, Jen's reacting, not planning. It's not smart, but facing danger makes you stay in the present."

Jonas wove strength and purpose into each minute. As Emily considered what he'd said, she thought about her fading sight. She had no idea what the future held, but today, he was there with her and she wasn't alone. *Now* was the time to create memories worthy of a lifetime.

AS THEY REACHED THE eastern outskirts of the community of Kirtland, they left the main road and followed Jen along what had once been the old highway. It led past farms, orchards and commuter housing areas created by the expansion of the city.

Soon Jen turned onto a dirt road that led south toward the river. The private road, poorly maintained, became extremely bumpy after they'd gone about a hundred yards. "Jen will need to slow down on this washboard road. That old SUV of hers is going to shake apart."

As he spoke, Jen pulled to a stop and got out. Moving quickly, she walked down a tree-lined lane and disappeared from view.

"Where did she go?" Emily asked, struggling to see in the half-light. Dusk made it nearly impossible for her to make out anything but muted shapes.

"Let's follow and find out."

Emily bit her lip worriedly. She wasn't sure she could find her way without tripping over something.

Almost as if he'd read her mind, Jonas added, "We'll stick together."

She nodded, still uneasy, but willing to trust him.

"We need to find out who she's meeting and, if possible, listen in on their conversation. I can't read lips in the dark."

Emily slid out of the truck on his side and took his hand. "I'm ready."

The sun had just set, and light was fading fast. She stuck close to Jonas as they walked along the rutted dirt road. Wearing canvas-and-leather cross-trainers, she was aware of the sandy ground beneath her feet and the smooth feel of packed gravel. Bringing all her senses to bear helped her maintain her balance—that, and Jonas's firm grip.

They'd been walking for a few minutes when she suddenly stopped and held up one hand. "Two people—a man and a woman—are speaking softly just ahead," she whispered.

"Let's move in closer."

"Go without me. You're trained for a silent approach, and are less likely to be spotted if you go by yourself." She was wearing a red jacket, but he was in faded jeans and a gray shirt, blending in perfectly with the low light. "I'll listen from here. I can hear them clearly enough."

As Jonas slipped away, she moved behind the cover of a tree and strained her ears. She was almost sure she recognized the man's voice, but couldn't quite place it.

"If he killed Robert, he'll come after me next. I know too much," she heard Jen say.

"He has something on us, we have something on him, so there's no reason to fall apart now. He's paid both of us well, and there's a lot more where that came from as long as we don't panic. Just don't give him the idea we can't be trusted," the man answered. "Money buys power, and he's got a hell of a lot more of both than we do. Just give me some time to feel out the situation."

"What should I do? Wait here at your house?" Jen asked.

"Yeah. He doesn't know about this place, and with me staying at that little cabin of his right now, there's no reason for him to look elsewhere. Just give me a day or two to see what's going on. We don't *know* it was him—not for sure. Sharks like Jefferson make all kinds of enemies."

"I still think we should take the money we have and get the heck out of here," Jen argued. "Waiting to see what he'll do next is just asking for trouble."

"Trust me, I'll be able to read him. I'll know if we're in danger. And he still owes me money."

Emily heard a vehicle start up. Thinking it would be coming her way, she squeezed closer to the tree. But the vehicle noise faded away instead of getting louder.

"I'm here," Jonas said, running up quickly. "We need to get to the truck in a hurry, and not just because Jen's coming back for her car. There's a second road that comes in from the east, and if we hurry, we can catch up to Sam by the time he passes by on the main highway." He grabbed Emily's hand and led her quickly back the way they'd come.

She didn't bother to look down, concentrating instead on keeping pace. "I couldn't place the guy's voice. It was familiar, and I know I've heard it before."

"It was Sam Carpenter," Jonas confirmed. "There's a small farmhouse at the other end of the field. Jen's not going anywhere once she hides her SUV, so we're going to stay on Sam's tail."

THEY REACHED THE JUNCTION at the main highway five minutes later, then waited, watching. Finally an old green pickup went by. "That's him," Jonas said. "Now, let's see where he goes."

"If we're reading this right, he'll turn south outside the city and head straight for Grant's place. The Woods family used to have a small guesthouse at the south end of the property. That could be the cabin he mentioned."

Fifteen minutes later, Sam's truck made the turn south. "Looks like you called it, Em."

"This still doesn't add up for me. Grant wants my land. He's made no secret of that. So why all the games? And why kill my real-estate attorney? I'm sure Robert would have preferred for me to sell to Grant. Since Grant would have needed to outbid the tribe for that southern parcel, that would have meant an even higher commission for Robert."

"Jefferson might have pushed himself into the game. Maybe he knew something Grant didn't want anyone else to know. Or he could have threatened to sour any offer Grant made you unless he got a kickback." Jonas expelled his breath in a hiss. "But something tells me we're still missing a vital piece."

"And how does Dinétsoh play into this? Grant couldn't have known about the bearer bonds, could he?"

"No, and that's what doesn't make sense." Jonas shook his head. His search yesterday had been fruitless, but others had kept looking for signs of their fellow warrior, even expanding their efforts beyond the Atkins property. Yet they'd found nothing.

Focusing on Sam, he forced himself to hold back. There was only one direct route to the Atkins-Woods turnoff, so there was no need to go in closer and risk alerting the man.

They soon rounded the last curve before reaching the western edge of Emily's land. Although Jonas had expected to pick up the glow of Sam's taillights immediately, there was nothing ahead. The vehicle was nowhere in sight.

"Where the heck is he?" Jonas pulled off the road and turned off his headlights, hoping to spot the pickup by the glint of chrome off the moonlight.

Visually, she couldn't help. To her, what lay beyond the truck's headlights was a blur of gray and black shadows. Without another option, Emily decided to rely on her hearing. Rolling down the window, she listened. A few minutes went by, then she heard something.

"There's another vehicle coming up behind us, and the engine sounds like Sam's pickup," she reported.

"He probably doused his lights, then turned off the road and waited until we passed by," Jonas said. "Let's use his own strategy against him. I'm going to cut across the road and find better cover down in the trees until *he* goes by. The we'll get back on his tail, even if we have to run without headlights. I don't want him behind us."

Within seconds they were across the road, in hiding. They listened, but the sound she'd heard had now faded. Although she tried, she couldn't hear anything except the faint ticking sound of their own engine as it cooled.

"Do you hear anything?" Jonas asked at last.

"No," she whispered. "Maybe I made a mistake. It could have been another pickup, not Sam's, and it turned off and went elsewhere."

"Or maybe Sam stopped and is waiting *us* out. Let's sit it out for a while longer," Jonas said.

Emily concentrated, but heard nothing out of the ordinary as the minutes passed. "Do you think he noticed us following him after he left Kirtland? If he was one of the two who raided my place, he knows what your truck looks like. He might have purposely led us here, pulled off, let us pass, then headed back in the opposite direction."

"If he did, we'll never find him now," Jonas stated. "But we can't assume anything. It's possible he never saw us and was just on his guard, taking precautions after his conversation with Jen."

As the moon rose high in the sky, Emily's vision improved slightly. "We've lost him," she said, mirroring his thoughts. "Let's go home. If possible, I'd like to check and see if my construction people made any progress today."

"How much are you really able to see in this light?" he asked, picking up on the way she'd phrased things.

She didn't answer right away and they continued in silence as he pulled out onto the highway. He looked over as they turned off on the long graveled road that led to her property, but she still avoided eye contact.

"It's hard to explain," she said at last. "There's a section of my field of vision that doesn't work at all, but I can get by with what's left. Details aren't always easy to see but—"

Jonas suddenly stomped down on the accelerator, and the truck fishtailed wildly. The next instant he braked hard. A gunshot exploded in the air as they slid to a stop in a cloud of dust. Another earsplitting crack followed, shaking the truck and shattering the windshield.

Jonas threw himself over Emily, pushing her onto the seat. As he did, pain gripped her and a burning sensation arrowed down from her shoulder to her wrist.

"Stay down!" he yelled.

Jonas pulled out his pistol, firing two quick shots through the shattered windshield, aiming in the direction the gunfire had come from.

Then, ducking low again, he checked her out quickly. "There's glass all over your face. Don't blink or try to rub with your hands. Raise up just enough to look down and shake off the fragments."

As she did so, most of the splinters fell away. When she reached up to try and brush away the bits that remained, small glass pieces fell into her sleeves and she cried out.

"Are you hit?" he asked immediately, his face inches from hers as he looked into her eyes. "Where does it hurt?"

"My arms," she managed to gasp. She could smell the sweet scent of blood and even taste some on her lips. Worst of all, she couldn't stop shaking.

He checked her over as well as he could while staying below window level. "The first round passed through both our windows. I could almost feel it go by. You were hit by the spray of glass from the windshield after the second shot, and you've got a lot of tiny cuts."

The engine was still running, so he turned off the ignition and doused the headlights, then raised his head slightly and looked out into the night. "He knows I can shoot back, but he might still be out there, waiting for us to show ourselves again. When I tell you, crawl out on my side, using the truck for cover. Then run off the road and into the brush. Stay low."

Something in his tone alerted her. "Where are you going?"

"After the sniper."

"In the dark? Are you crazy?"

"I'm trained to fight at night, and that's one advantage I intend to use." He opened the driver's side door and slipped out. Taking a position near the hinges, pistol up, he aimed across the hood.

"Don't go. It's too dangerous," she said. "There could be more than one gunman out there."

"He missed both of us, so he's not an expert. I am." Jonas urged her out. "Run for the trees. I'll cover you. Now go!" He fired two shots as she ran off the road and into the brush.

Alone in her hiding place beneath a willow moments later, Emily heard him move off, melding into the darkness. She shook her sweater, loosening small chunks of glass that had been cutting into her skin. A few pieces had even managed to work their way through her collar opening.

Leaning forward, she pulled her shirt away from her body and shook them loose, but as she did, other small fragments bit into her. There were too many to simply brush off. What she needed now was a shower and a lot of disinfectant—assuming she made it home.

"I couldn't catch him," a voice behind her said.

Emily nearly jumped out of her skin.

"I'm sorry. I thought you heard me coming back. I wasn't being quiet," Jonas added, touching her on the shoulder lightly.

"I can hear the leaves rustling, but you don't make any sound at all when you walk."

"Sorry about that," he said. "It's a skill I learned, one useful in staying alive, and somewhere along the way it became a part of me." In the moonlight he could see the small cuts on her forearm and neck. "You're going to have to get out of those clothes and clean those cuts."

"If it's safe now, take me home. I'll dust myself off with a dry cloth, then take a shower." And maybe, just maybe, she'd finally escape the scent of death that still clung to her.

JONAS BRUSHED AWAY THE glass inside the cab so she could safely sit down again. Then, after making a quick call, they got under way.

Fixing his eyes on the road, he tried to bite back the anger blasting through him. This was his fault. He'd been distracted and hadn't seen or heard the threat soon enough. They'd been lucky that the sniper's own incompetence had given him away.

Snipers at night were particularly dangerous. This one had hidden well, but the truck's headlights had bounced off the rifle's optics, creating a flash of light. Though Jonas only had a second to accelerate, it had been enough to throw off the kill shot. The sniper had been forced to settle for driving a round through the windshield.

The shooter had targeted Emily, and Jonas had already called his contact to report the details. Preston Jim, another Brotherhood warrior, would be watching the farmhouse where Jen Caldwell was staying, just in case she, too, was about to become a target.

This close call just went to prove that Jonas's feelings were getting in the way of his judgment. Whenever he was around Emily, too many other thoughts crowded his mind. The softness of her curves, the warmth of her voice, the way her hips swayed when she walked, filled him with a need that never went away. Denying it only left him feeling like half a man—one torn between duty and the need to lose himself in her, completing her, completing himself.

Even now, the thought made him harden. Disgusted with himself, he managed only two words. "I'm sorry."

She looked at him in surprise. "For what?"

"For failing to protect you."

"You sped up, then hit the brakes, throwing off the sniper. After that, you placed your body between me and danger. There was nothing else you could have done," she answered. "I still haven't figured out how you knew the gunman was there."

"The gleam of the scope in the headlights. But by then it was almost too late. I should have been looking harder, expecting an ambush. I screwed up, and you could have been killed."

"I'm alive because of you. If you hadn't forced me down…" She shook her head. "I'm the one who's to blame here, not you."

"You, how?" he asked, surprised.

"At night everything fades and all I see are dark shapes. I should have made that very clear to you long before now, so you wouldn't count on me to help you keep a lookout. But I let you down," she said. "And every day my sight gets a little worse."

"Are you going blind?"

"Unless a cure is found, or gene therapy works, probably. I didn't tell you before because I didn't want you to feel sorry for me. It was pride, but you deserved better."

Jonas reached for her hand and entwined his fingers with hers.

She held on to him tightly. With Jonas, she felt vibrantly feminine, and desired. That knowledge was like a bright liquid fire coursing through her, pushing back the fears that shadowed her.

"You could never let me down," he said, fighting to quell feelings that were too strong, too raw, to release. "After months of living on the edge, I didn't think I was capable of falling in love. But I was wrong."

His words were the song her heart had longed for. Jonas wasn't offering her pity—he was giving her the greatest gift of all.

She turned in her seat to face him, but as she did, more glass particles tore into her skin. She cried out and looked down at herself. "I'm bleeding again," she noted in a shaky voice.

He focused on his driving, making sure to miss every bump he could. "Once we arrive, strip down."

Even as he said it, his body hardened. Cursing himself, he glanced over at her, and felt a surge of protectiveness that transcended his own needs.

"Deployed overseas, I learned that there's a trick to dealing with pain," he said, his voice taut. "Fill your mind with something that gives you intense pleasure—images that require you to use all your senses."

As Emily looked at him, he saw her mouth part and her gaze soften. It was a look any man worth his salt could recognize. Raw heat blasted through him. "Hold on to those thoughts, Em. If you do, there won't be any room for pain."

Chapter Sixteen

Jonas paced restlessly in the small trailer. He'd learned to remain immobile for hours during a mission, but sitting still was beyond him now. He'd walked Emily to the bathroom and, at her request, left her alone, giving her the privacy she'd asked for. He could have tried to convince her to let him stay, but distractions had taken enough of a toll—on him and on her.

He went to the window and checked outside, but all was quiet now. The only sound he could hear was the shower in the tiny bathroom. Though a door separated them, he was attuned to her movements. He heard her turn off the water and reach for a towel.

A heartbeat later he heard her cry out, and was instantly at the door. "What's wrong?"

"There's a sliver of glass stuck in my side. I can't see it or reach it, but it's there."

"Let me help," he said, and pulled the door open before she could protest.

She was standing with a towel draped in front of her, her expression a mixture of vulnerability and apprehension. Even without makeup, her beauty nearly tore his breath away.

"I can't wrap the towel all the way around. The glass…" she said, still trying to find a way to cover up.

"What are you worried about?" he asked in a tortured whisper. "I've seen you…and felt you…before. Or have you forgotten?"

She shivered, and seeing her respond to him, though he hadn't even touched her, drove him to the edge. Passion and desire clawed at his gut, but he forced himself to clamp a firm lid on that. This was about helping Emily—it wasn't about him.

"Turn around and let me see if I can help."

As she did so, exposing herself to his gaze, his body became rock hard. He sucked in a ragged breath and collected every last shred of self-control he possessed. Touching her gently, he ran his hand over the cut and pulled out the small sliver of glass, then helped her put antiseptic on her scratches, which weren't as bad as she'd thought. "You're okay now," he said when they were close.

She turned to face him. "Thank you, Jonas." Standing on tiptoe, she brushed his lips with a tender kiss.

He stood still, barely allowing himself to kiss her back.

"Are you angry about something?" she asked, wrapping the towel in place.

"Not even close," he said, his voice taut. "What I'm feeling right now…" He shook his head. "I want you, Em, and I'm too wound up. Stay safe—keep your distance."

Emily drew a deep breath. She'd spent too much time being cautious and planning everything. It was time to let go. The passion, the exquisite tenderness and pleasures of love—that was Life with a capital *L*. She took a step closer to him.

"I'm not afraid of you. Go ahead. Show me what's in your heart, Jonas," she challenged softly.

Acting on instinct alone, he pulled the towel away and, hauling her against him, kissed her hard.

With a whimper, she tugged at his shirt, pushing it away from his shoulders. "I need to feel you, to taste you."

Her words blasted through him. She was struggling with his belt, and, bringing his hands over hers, he helped.

Clothing cast away in a heap, he pulled her back into his arms.

"No more secrets," Emily said, her hands torturing him with tender caresses that drove him to that ragged edge.

Reaching into himself for the last bit of sanity, Jonas drew back and gazed into her eyes. "Some secrets are not mine to tell."

She brought his lips down to hers, kissed him, then whispered, "I've known who and what you are for some time. Dinétsoh told my dad about the Brotherhood and those who took the oath. I overheard—but I never told a soul—until now." She rubbed her body against his, heat to heat.

"Then the night belongs to us."

Though he'd spoken only of this night, she accepted his terms, and gave herself to him. "Make it last," Emily whispered as he lifted her off her feet and carried her to the bed.

"No lights," he said, turning off the lamp, then setting her on the mattress. "Tonight we'll share the dark, and find each other in ways no one else ever could. Close your eyes, *sawe,* and just feel," he murmured in her ear.

The night became a journey of textures and sensations, each more intense than the last. He gently stroked her skin, exploring her body, and the familiar and exciting roughness of his work-hardened hands sent shivers of pleasure coursing through her.

Caressing her in ways meant to drive her wild, and whispering erotic words into her ear, he took her to the brink and beyond, again and again. When he was satisfied that she could give him no more, he held her against him, waiting for her to gather her strength.

At long last, she shifted and, letting instinct guide her, positioned herself over him. He'd driven her wild, and now she would do the same for him. She wanted to shatter his control, to drive him to that dark edge where there was no room for restraint. Before the night was through she wanted him wild in her arms. Any woman who was a woman had that power over her man. Tonight would be a journey of discovery—for him, for her.

"I want you to remember tonight—and me—forever," she murmured, leaning down to nip at his earlobe. Straddling him so he could feel her heat, she rubbed herself sensuously against him as she moved along his length, trailing moist kisses.

He was all heat and power, rolled into one masculine package. When she took him into her mouth, he snapped. With a wild growl, he drew her up roughly, and kissed her in a way that branded her as his.

Her small whimpers added fuel to the fire in his veins. He'd never get enough. He forced her back onto the mattress, gripped her hands and thrust inside her, burying himself in her. Blood thundered through him as he rode her. Hearing her cries drove him crazy. He angled her hips so he could penetrate even deeper.

Each thrust brought him closer, but he held on until she bucked beneath him and he felt her come apart. Blind with passion, he followed her into that oblivion, filling her with himself.

Sanity returned slowly as the night stretched out before them. "Am I too heavy?" he asked at last, his voice nothing more than a low rumble.

"No. I feel…complete."

Her voice caressed him in the darkness of the room. "And the night's just beginning," he said, kissing her gently.

"The darkness…held surprises."

"It allowed us a new way to see…and feel." He ran his hand down her body and caressed the pulse point at her center.

She gasped and arched against him. "I can't."

"Yes, you can." Showing her exquisite tenderness this time, he gave her everything, then entered her again.

THE SUN COMING IN through the pale curtains nudged her awake. She opened her eyes slowly and saw Jonas approaching the bed, cup of coffee in hand.

"Here you go, sleepyhead. It's freshly brewed."

He was already dressed, and as she sat up, she suddenly became aware of her own nakedness. She pulled up the sheet quickly.

"*Sawe,* there's nothing you've got that I haven't seen, touched or tasted," he said, his voice deep. "There's no room for modesty between us anymore."

He brushed a kiss on her forehead. "Now get up. There's work to be done. I have to go back to the area where I lost the sniper."

She nearly choked on the coffee. Of places she never wanted to revisit, that was up there near the top of the list.

"Why go back? He's long gone," she protested.

"Yes, undoubtedly, but his trail's still there and I'm going to find it. When it comes to tracking, I'm the best there is."

"That's the quality I love most about you," she said with a hint of a smile.

"That I won't give up?"

"No, your humility."

He burst out laughing. "Get dressed, woman. We need to check that road before the workers' vehicles wipe out any of the trail."

They were under way ten minutes later, and as they drove to the site, Jonas lapsed into a tense silence.

"What's wrong?" she asked.

He started to deny that anything was, then changed his mind. "What went on between us last night—we can't let it happen again."

"You regret it?" Emily's heart stopped cold, and for a moment she couldn't even draw a breath.

"No," he answered, his voice gruff. "I have no regrets. We both needed each other, and what happened was…right. But my life and yours—don't mix."

She swallowed, determined to keep her voice as steady and detached as his had been. "We're both in agreement then. No promises were made, and none need to be kept."

As she swallowed hard to avoid tears, she was glad that his

attention was on the road. Life had taught her that people came—
and left. Her mom, her dad…Jonas. That was just the way things
were, and she couldn't change it. *Nothing* was forever.

JONAS FOCUSED ON THE road, looking for the spot where they'd
been ambushed. He wouldn't fail her—and himself—again.

"The sniper fired from your side," he stated, as they pulled
up to the site. "I wasn't able to determine if he'd crossed the
road before or after, so we don't know which route he took into
the area, or how he left."

"Let's get out and take a closer look around," Emily suggested.

They left the truck parked off the road, then walked on for
about a hundred yards before heading up the hillside. The
ground here was mostly weathered sandstone, hard enough not
to show clear footprints, but easily scuffed.

"The shooter took aim from here," Jonas said. "I saw the
muzzle flash, and the swerve marks we left down on the road
support that." He crouched and searched the ground. "He left
no shell casings behind."

"So we know he's careful and picks up after himself," she
noted.

"Yes, even with me shooting back. But, admittedly, I was
aiming low, not wanting the bullets to hit something a mile
away. My primary goal was to suppress his fire," he said. "What
we need to do now is spiral out and search the area. But play
it safe and stay close to cover, and watch out for signs of a
trap—not just an ambush. If you see or hear anything, let me
know right away."

Determined to be of some use, Emily brought all her senses
into full play. The air was crisp and clean, and there was a faint
trace of smoke coming from someone's fireplace. She stopped
in midstride and listened. Just beyond the cry of a hawk
soaring overhead, another sharp, crisp sound drifted in on the
morning breeze.

He stopped when she did, and looked over at her, waiting.

"Do you hear it?" she asked quietly. "It's the sound of metal against metal."

He listened, then shook his head. "Are you sure?"

"Yes. It's coming from that direction, across the road to the east." She pointed. "Let's go check it out."

They'd reached the road and were crossing when he also heard it—a metallic crunch, like something cutting steel. He recognized it from operations where mines were laid and trip wires prepared. There was another sound, too, a rhythmic hammering—as if stakes were being driven into the ground. Now that he could hear it, it didn't take him long to pinpoint the location.

He led the way confidently, motioning for Emily to stay low and silent as they worked their way diagonally up a rise on Grant's side of the road. As they drew near, Jonas stopped behind some brush near the crest of the hill. Crouched behind thin cover, he pointed to the area below, where two men were working on a fence line leading up to Grant Woods's gate.

Using the small binoculars he'd brought, Jonas studied the scene. It was Grant and Sam Carpenter, wearing work clothes and heavy gloves. They had a variety of tools and a wire stretcher, and were repairing the fence.

Jonas focused on the tarp strewn on the ground several feet from a two-wheeled yard cart. Two rifles, one the Marlin .22 they'd seen Carpenter with the other day, and the other a Ruger Mini-14 with a scope, lay on the protective canvas.

Although Jonas still had no proof, he now had a real good idea who'd taken a shot at them the night before. He'd been unable to find the round that had taken out the windshield. But he knew the crack of a center-fire cartridge, especially a .22, and his money was on the Ruger, which was available in that caliber. The question that remained was who'd carried it last night.

Jonas studied their adversaries, who were less than fifty

yards away. Although he wanted to move in closer, he wouldn't risk Emily again.

As he glanced back at her and their eyes met, all the disciplines he'd learned as a member of the Brotherhood of Warriors faded momentarily. Angry with himself, he looked away and focused again on the men. He was acting like a fool, and in a life and death situation, there was no room for mistakes.

Used to remaining perfectly still for hours if need be, he kept a steady watch. What surprised him was Emily's ability to do the same. She uttered no complaint as the minutes ticked by.

Soon, Sam loaded up the tools and tarp, and handed Grant the Ruger. Placing the .22 in the cart, he picked up the handles and wheeled it off in the direction of Grant's house, following the furrows left on the journey out.

Without a backward glance at his handyman, Grant checked the magazine on the Ruger, then walked out his gate. Jonas and Emily ducked low, watching, as her neighbor crossed the road and climbed uphill onto Emily's land.

"Come on. We're following Grant," Jonas whispered, intending on staying well back. Emily was his priority, and he didn't want to expose her to any unnecessary danger.

"Shouldn't we get your rifle from the truck?" she asked. "He has one."

"If we go back, we could lose him," he said. "But don't worry. I intend to avoid a shootout."

She followed him down the hill, moving as quietly as she could.

Although he'd kept a sharp eye on his target, the terrain was undulating, the junipers low and thick, and the ground hard. Before long, Jonas knew he'd lost Grant's trail.

"He's up ahead somewhere, but I can't hear him moving at all." Jonas tuned in to the area around them. "Change of plans. We're getting out of here right now."

"What's wrong?" she asked quickly.

"I'm getting bad vibes. First Grant heads into some rough terrain, and now he's nowhere in sight. My gut tells me we're being set up. Stay close to me, and keep checking the ground for his tracks while I keep watch around our perimeter. We're heading back."

Jonas chose a circuitous route toward the road, moving in a parallel course instead of retracing their steps. He could hunt, but he also knew how to evade. Between his Ranger training in the military and his experience with the Brotherhood, he knew all the tricks of the trade.

He chose the way carefully—watching, listening, taking the higher ground to give themselves the advantage. His concentration was absolute. One moment's distraction could result in lethal consequences. Images flashed in his mind. His buddy, Marc, the explosion, the choking scent of burned flesh, and a road covered in torn limbs and blood.

Jonas shook free of the thought. He knew how to stay alive, and that's why he was here now instead of in a cemetery on the Navajo Nation. Without focus, they would be nothing more than the walking dead out here.

Gun in hand, he continued. The world needed warriors who could fight the good fight, and he was the best of the best. Though he'd tried hard to deny it, there was no place for love in his life. That softened a man and muddied his objectivity. Ignoring the hollow feeling in his gut, he pressed on.

Chapter Seventeen

"Look," Emily said, pointing to a set of footprints in the packed clay that separated two sandstone bedrock layers. Though days old, they were still distinctive enough to make out. "Those tracks could be Dinétsoh's. Is it possible he circled around after the accident, trying to lose whoever was after him?"

"It's more likely he was backtracking. Tactically speaking, the bluffs would have been a better defensive position."

She moved in that direction, then stopped after reaching the next layer of sandstone. "The trail—it's gone. No, wait—what's that?" Emily stooped to examine a nearly black spot on the stone, then suddenly recoiled. "I think it may be dried blood," she said, her memory flashing back to what she'd seen in the motel room.

He verified it with just one glance. In the desert, blood usually dried a glossy black, then cracked. He looked around for more. "It's possible the blood belongs to Dinétsoh, but it's also likely that it was left by an injured animal, and the footprints belong to a hunter tracking wounded prey."

Jonas wanted to stay and look around, but it wasn't an option right now. He studied the terrain, then took one last glance at the footprints. His mentor would have known to step around or over the soft ground. Those tracks either were not Dinétsoh's—or he'd left them there on purpose.

If that was the case, perhaps there was something else to see. Jonas studied the ground. A broken branch lay a few feet from where he stood. Between the leaves, he could see a pattern on the surface of the sandstone. Curious, he crouched down and carefully parted the leaves. One word—*sih*—had been scratched into the surface of the rock with a piece of hard quartzite, which was still lying there.

"What's it mean?" she asked.

"It's Navajo. It means 'chance' or 'life.'"

"Then it's a message from Dinétsoh," she said, mirroring his thoughts.

Before he could answer, he heard a pair of doves take flight from the rim of a shallow wash to their right. Knowing that doves rarely fled unless danger was almost upon them, he immediately took action. "We're being tailed. Let's move."

"Grant? Or Sam?"

"Sam couldn't have caught up with us this soon. I think Grant hid out as we passed and is now following us. My guess is he's paralleling our route. You and I need to head uphill double-time and put some distance between us and this," he said, pointing to the ground, then eradicating the mark. "I don't want either of those men to see what we've found."

Jonas focused on the path ahead, trying to find a route that would put their back to the cliffs so they couldn't be trapped in a crossfire. Calling for backup was an option, but he knew help would take time to arrive, and Emily and he would be hard to locate on the move. It could also end up leading friendly forces into an ambush.

"If he catches up, I need you to do exactly what I tell you. No hesitation, no arguments. Anything else might get us both killed."

"All right," she answered, breathing hard from the pace. "Do you think Sam and Grant are closing in on us?"

"Right now, instinct tells me to stay low and move fast."

It wasn't a direct answer, but she understood. He sensed trouble in much the same way that she could feel an approaching storm.

They soon reached the lower slopes of the bluffs. Here, boulders the size of refrigerators were scattered around like children's blocks, and at the base of the cliffs themselves, more were poised to tumble down during the next millennium.

Although there were several trails they could use to climb, he needed a route that wouldn't readily expose them to anyone below. Finally choosing the path that would give them the most cover, he led the way.

She followed, doing her best not to get entangled in the brush, and although she wasn't always successful, she kept up.

"Maybe no one's back there," she said, after minutes passed and nothing happened.

"There is," he assured her, his voice barely a whisper. "We'll need to cross that open slope to reach that saddle between the high points," he added, gesturing ahead. "Stay low and move fast. And no matter what happens, keep going forward until you reach that pile of boulders."

They were halfway across, scrambling on loose gravel, when a couple of rifle shots rang out and bullets whined overhead.

"Don't stop!" he yelled. Grabbing her hand, he took off running in a random, zigzag pattern toward their goal—the big boulders.

Three more bullets flew past them, ricocheting off rocks to the right of Emily.

Acting on instinct, Jonas urged her to zig in that direction, and a half second later, another bullet struck the ground to their left.

Ten feet from cover, Jonas dived, pulling Emily along. They hit the packed ground hard, but now they were behind a sandstone boulder the size of a desk.

"Stay down." Jonas rose to his knees, peered around the side of the rock and squeezed off a shot.

A standing figure below, aiming a rifle, dived to the ground. From the clothing, Jonas thought it was Grant, but he couldn't be sure at this distance.

"Easy target if I'd brought the rifle," he grumbled.

Emily crawled up behind him, but wisely didn't take a look. A bullet nicked the top of the rock, then struck something behind them with a thump.

She glanced over her shoulder. "What now? There's a mine shaft back there, I think, but it's boarded up."

Jonas studied the area. They were atop a weathered shelflike platform carved out of the cliff, and behind them were a half-dozen graying boards flat on the ground. "All those shafts should connect to the main tunnels and lead to another opening elsewhere or on top of the mesa. That could be our safest way up."

"Those mines are anything but safe."

"Beats being easy rifle targets. I'm going over there to pull away the timbers. While I'm exposed, you'll need to keep the sniper busy." He gave her his pistol. "Stay low and aim out from ground level. Just don't let any dirt get into the barrel. Shoot toward the rocks between the closest trees. Fire quickly, then duck back. It doesn't matter if you don't hit anything. All I need you to do is keep him down."

"No, let's just wait him out. He can't come after us here, and he won't cross that open stretch because he knows you won't miss at that distance. If you and I go into those mines, we'll either fall or get lost," she said, remembering all the cautions she'd heard growing up. The tunnels held only death for the uninvited.

Another shot ricocheted off the rocks. Jonas pulled her even lower. "We can't stay. Once his partner arrives, one of them will keep us pinned while the other advances. Trust me, and do as I ask. Just squeeze the trigger. Make it quick and random. Change your location slightly when you shoot, too, and alter your timing. That way he won't know when your next shot's going to be or where you'll pop up."

As soon as she fired the first shot, he moved away, crawling on his stomach toward the boards.

It took him only seconds to pull the heavy, rotting boards away from the opening, because someone else had pried them loose before. They'd been laid back in place, not fastened, over the three-foot-diameter hole.

The ventilation shaft or emergency exit he uncovered was wide enough to squeeze through. There was even a wooden ladder, and it looked sturdy enough to support them. The absence of spiderwebs indicated that someone else had used this entrance not long ago, also an encouraging sign.

"Take one more shot to make him think, then run over," he whispered harshly.

As she reached his position, he took the pistol and urged her down the makeshift ladder ahead of him. The pitch-blackness inside was daunting, but they were out of options.

"There's a ledge where the ladder stops. No, wait, I think it's the bottom. There are wooden supports on the walls," she said.

He'd been following her, holding on with one hand and keeping the pistol aimed up toward the opening. "Step away so he can't shoot down at you. I'll be there in a moment."

Jonas took the next several rungs in a hurry, then stepped off beside her. The "skylight" didn't offer much light, but it was clear they were at the bottom of the hole. The horizontal shaft, leading in two opposite directions and perhaps tracing the route of the former coal seam into the hillside, was nearly five feet high. In places, heavy timbers had been installed to support the tunnel.

Jonas replaced the almost-empty pistol magazine with a fully loaded one by touch, something he could do in his sleep. Then he pulled out the penlight he carried in his pocket. It was better than nothing, but barely. The darkness seemed to absorb the tiny beam, closing in on it, strangling its muted light.

Though he tried to peer down both tunnels, the small beam revealed nothing beyond twenty feet.

"We can't stay here," he said quickly. "The shooter could pick us off too easily. Go to your right. I think that tunnel's wider."

She stood motionless for a moment. "No. We need to go to our left." In the semidarkness, her heightened senses would be her best guides. "There's another way out at that end. Don't you *feel* it?"

"Feel what?" he asked, his gaze still on the opening above.

Before she could answer, they both heard running footsteps at the top of the shaft, and a board being tossed aside. "One man," Emily whispered. "But who? Grant?"

Jonas took a quick look up, then stepped back into hiding, nodding. Handing Emily the light, he motioned toward the left tunnel and followed her, covering the rear and listening for footsteps on the ladder.

The rock sides and the darkness conspired together, undermining her courage with each step. It was like being buried alive. What kept her going was the scent of hope. "There's fresh air coming from the other end of this tunnel."

He listened as her voice rose with excitement, and didn't have the heart to tell her that didn't guarantee the opening would be big enough for them to use. Mines were often complex mazes with multiple air shafts and exits. If the next opening was partially collapsed, they'd have to continue searching, hoping that the other former exits hadn't caved in or were otherwise inaccessible.

As they continued, their route slanting downhill slightly, he remained focused on protecting their rear. If the shooter decided to come in after them, there wouldn't be much room to maneuver. Jonas's pistol was a better weapon than a rifle in tight spaces, but firing any weapon in these tunnels could be an act of suicide. A sudden loud sound could collapse the ceilings, which had only a few supporting timbers. Hopefully, whoever was after them would have enough sense to know that, too.

What worried him most now was the possibility the gunman already knew where the closest exit was, and was moving on to ambush them when they came out.

Emily placed her hand on the stone wall for balance, then suddenly pulled it back. "There's some kind of powder on the rock face. Is it coal dust? I heard that's explosive."

He took the penlight from her hand and shone it where she indicated. "Not coal, it's white powder..." He touched it, then rubbed his fingertips together. "It feels like pollen and white shell—the contents of a medicine bundle. Dinétsoh came this way," he said, new hope restoring his energy.

He aimed the light toward the floor, which was coated with a fine layer of dust. "No footprints, so he must have rubbed them out as he went."

As the tunnel straightened again, she saw light streaming into the section ahead. "If Dinétsoh made it back out of the mine, we can, too."

He studied the ground carefully, taking advantage of the extra light. "Maybe he stayed inside. This tunnel joins up with what appears to be a natural cave," he said, looking ahead and pointing to the rough, high ceiling, devoid of any supporting timbers. The walls hadn't been cut into, and had kept their natural shape.

"I think that's where he went," he said, remembering what he'd been told about Fire Rock Hollow.

"Is there any way for us to tell for sure?" she asked, trying to see what he did, but not having much luck.

"There's a faint set of footprints leading in there." Stepping over to the passage, he crouched and aimed the light to the floor of the cavern. "There's more dried blood here, too."

"Let's go then," she said. "If he managed to stay alive, he'll need help."

Jonas looked down at the ground again and shook his head. "According to this second set of tracks, he came back out. The exit print overlays one that leads in."

"Then where is he now?" she asked, wishing she could see in the dim light.

"He may have gone down another tunnel and fallen into a vertical shaft, or even found a route out farther east or west. But the chances of him being alive after so many days aren't good." Jonas suddenly stopped speaking and put his finger over his lips. There was a faint echo of footsteps coming from the tunnel they'd taken.

"We can't stay here," he said. "Head for the light and take the first exit possible."

About fifty feet down the largest mine shaft, they found a pile of rubble, and a big gap at the top, leading outside. "I'll go up first and check things out," Jonas said, handing her his pistol. "Watch behind us."

Emily heard him climb out, and then it was dead silent. In that stillness it felt as if the darkness of the tunnels was calling to her, whispering to a kindred spirit who'd one day live in the dark.

Seconds turned into eternities until, at long last, she heard a noise above her. Glancing up, she saw Jonas on his knees, motioning to her.

She climbed up the loose rubble, picking her way across the sharp rocks, and emerged into the sunlight. Breathing a sigh of relief, she made herself a promise. She would never go underground again.

Suddenly remembering Dinétsoh, she felt her chest tighten. "We'll have to go back in as soon as we can. Dinétsoh might still be in one of those tunnels. We can't be one hundred percent sure until we check."

"We'll come back, but right now we have to get away from here."

"Do you know where we are?" she asked, scanning the hillside.

"I recognize the general area," he said, leading the way down the slope. "We're above Grant's property." He pointed off to their right. "That looks like a roof over there, about a half mile away. It must be the cabin Sam was working on. We'll head there next."

"At least we now know why Jen and Sam were worried about Grant. From the looks of it, Grant was the one who killed Jefferson, and probably my father," Emily said. "But why is he risking everything for my land? He has enough of his own."

"Maybe Sam and Jen can tell us more."

Chapter Eighteen

Jonas pulled out his cell phone as they proceeded. After making a quick call, he glanced over at her. "I told the man watching the house where Jen Caldwell is holed up to get the sheriff's department over there immediately. She's a material witness to the Jefferson murder now, and I don't want Woods to catch up to her first."

"That's not very likely. He's after us at the moment."

Hearing Emily's voice waver, he reached for her hand. "It's been a long road, Em. Don't stop believing in me."

As she glanced into the dark depths of his eyes, she saw determination, and another, gentler emotion that took her breath away. The Brotherhood had his loyalty, but she had his heart. "We'll see this through together."

He smiled, pleased. "Now let's go find Sam Carpenter and offer him the chance to take down his boss."

When they were close to the cabin, Jonas slowed his pace and signaled her to crouch. Lifting his binoculars, he studied the small, wood-framed structure.

"There's a pickup out front, and it looks like the one we followed last night," he said.

"Is anyone in sight?"

"Yes, Sam just came out of the cabin. Now he's pacing back

and forth between the truck and the entrance, cell phone to his ear. He looks angry. There's a rifle on the front step."

"What now?"

"I'm going down there and taking him out. Once it's safe, I'll signal you to join me," Jonas said.

"No, wait. What if—" The rest of that thought was too awful to contemplate, and the words got jammed at the back of her throat.

"Don't worry. This is what I do. Nobody's going to die—especially me. Just stay down and wait for my all clear." He paused, pulled out a pen and wrote something on a page of a small notebook. "If Grant shows up, or something goes wrong, do *not* come to help me. Take off, hide, then call this number and ask for help." He handed her the paper.

"I will not 'take off,'" she said angrily. "How could you even think I'd run away and abandon you?"

He expelled a breath and shook his head. "I'm here to keep you safe—"

"Then you better keep yourself safe."

"All right," he muttered, exasperated. "Stay here until you hear from me. Can I count on you to do that?"

"For now. But maybe I can help."

"How?"

"Once you're in position and ready to jump him, give me a buzz on my cell phone. I'll yell and wave. When he looks over at me..."

"I make my move," he finished with a nod. "Okay, you're the diversion. But hit the ground if he reaches for his rifle."

"Deal."

Jonas moved silently, and she waited under cover. About five minutes later, her cell phone vibrated. Swallowing hard, she stepped out in the open and yelled, "Hey, Sam! Where's your boss?"

The man turned in surprise, stared a second, then stepped over to pick up his rifle.

Before he could reach it, Jonas dived out from behind the corner of the cabin and tackled him to the ground.

As the two men fought, each hoping to get to the rifle first, Emily raced toward them. By the time she arrived, the fight was over and Sam was on his knees. Jonas, aiming the rifle straight at him, and not taking his eyes off his prisoner, called out, "Okay, we're—"

"Don't shout. I'm here." Emily stopped about ten feet away. "Sorry. I couldn't wait."

She looked at Sam and saw the man was shaking. Something told her this was more than just a reaction to the fight he'd lost.

"You two can't stay here. He might see—" Sam's gaze darted around nervously. "Jen…"

"Is safe," Jonas finished for him.

"No, she's not. Grant has her. He just called me on the phone to gloat. But maybe he'll trade me for her."

"Wait—Grant has Jen?" Emily looked at Jonas. "How can that be?"

Jonas pulled out his pistol and leaned Sam's rifle against the wall. "Emily, call the number I gave you and check. Preston will know."

Emily brought out the piece of paper and her cell phone, then spoke hurriedly. Less than thirty seconds later, she closed the phone. "Preston says that he was about to call you. He heard that the TV was on, but when he went in closer to take a look, no one was inside."

"Grant's not stupid. He must have known you'd have someone keep an eye on her, and left the set on," Sam said, his voice rising. "You've underestimated him badly."

"He must have followed her—and us—to Kirtland," Jonas said, peeling his lips back in disgust.

"You're wasting time. I need to go—now," Sam said. "You don't know Grant."

"Do you think he'd hurt her?" Emily asked him.

"I can't predict him right now. He's feeling trapped. If he's tying up loose ends, he'll want me dead. But as for Jen..." He shook his head. "I think he'll keep her around and use her until he gets bored. Then he'll kill her. The best chance she's got is if I trade myself for her. But you have to let me go—now."

The sound of a single shot echoed against the bluffs, and Sam shuddered, grabbing his chest.

Jonas instantly yanked Emily into the cabin. "Down on the floor!"

Using the thick log walls for protection, he dropped to his knees beside the doorjamb and fired two quick shots up the road, in the direction the bullet had come from. He watched, hoping for return fire so he could get a fix on Grant's location, but nothing happened. A minute passed, then they heard the sound of a vehicle.

"Sam needs help." Emily scrambled to her feet and headed for the door.

Jonas grabbed her and pulled her back. "Stay inside. Sam's dead."

"What? No." She shook her head.

"He took a bullet through the heart. He was dead before he hit the ground."

Tears streamed down her face. "I can't do this anymore. My inn isn't worth anyone's life."

Jonas grasped her shoulders and forced her to look at him. "Em, this isn't about your inn—not anymore. This is about fighting for what's right. When good people look the other way and refuse to take action, evil gets the upper hand."

"But evil will always be around."

"It's true no one can destroy evil. It's a part of life and will always find a way to make itself felt. What we can do is bring it under control. That's what we're fighting for now—to restore the balance. Without that, everyone loses."

His words, rooted in the Navajo Way, reached her. She

gathered her courage, and making sure her voice remained steady, asked, "What's our next move? Should we go after Grant?"

She wasn't a warrior by trade, but she certainly had the heart of one. Knowing that she needed him more than ever sharpened his focus.

"The sniper, probably Grant, took off in a hurry. He wasn't interested in us," he said, stepping outside and looking down the road. A cloud of dust indicated the passage of a vehicle. "I think Sam was right. Grant's tying up loose ends."

Jonas flipped open his cell phone and spoke quickly in Navajo to Diné Nééz, asking that an area search be made to find Grant Woods, keeping an eye out for a possible hostage. After giving him a description of Jen, he hung up.

When he turned around, he saw Emily at Sam's laptop computer, which rested atop a small wooden table. "You need to see this," she said quietly, turning the screen so it faced him. "It was already on, open to a file named Security. Looks like Sam's been keeping records. He listed each of his and Jen's 'jobs' for Grant, and how much they were paid. The dates for his 'jobs' match the attacks on us, including last night. He also kept a log and mentions finding out that Jefferson tried to blackmail Woods." She turned her head and looked up. "Sam was eavesdropping and got caught," she finally concluded.

"Bad luck on his part," Jonas said, stepping close enough to read over her shoulder.

Emily nodded. "Sam and Jen knew too much about Grant for their own good. When Robert told Jen to research Grant's financial profile, she found out that he owns the company that holds my mortgage. When she told Jefferson, he realized that Grant was behind the sabotage on my inn. If I was forced to sell or default on the mortgage, Grant would get my place."

"So Jefferson tried to cut himself in, and Grant killed him," Jonas surmised. "Sam screwed up when he tried the same thing, pushing Grant for more money. But we're still missing something. None of this explains why your father was attacked, and what happened to Dinétsoh. This turned into a high-stakes game for Grant somewhere along the way. What we don't know is why. If we could figure out why buying you out was so important to him, I think we'd be able to put things together."

"There's nothing on my land that can explain this," she said flatly. "But we can't stop to figure it out right now. We have to find Jen. I doubt Grant would hide her at his house. It's too obvious. So where do we look?"

"Search Sam's other files. Maybe one of them will give us a lead," he said.

When a quick scan of the other data files produced nothing, Jonas looked down at the menu on the screen. "Call up his graphic files. There could be photos of Grant's property there, maybe even the place where he's hiding Jen."

Emily opened the folder and stared at the thumbnail images. "Here are several candid snapshots of Jen. But the ones at the bottom…" She shuddered as she glanced at the images of the young woman tied to a chair. "She looks terrified."

"Enlarge those photos, focusing on the background," he said.

Emily did as he asked, and swallowed as more graphic details came into view. "Grant hasn't had Jen for very long. How could these have been taken already, and how did Sam find them so quickly?"

"That's not Jen," Jonas answered. "That's someone else who looks a lot like her. From the quality of those photos I suspect they were taken years ago with a cheap camera, then scanned in later. This might be the secret Grant's willing to kill to protect."

"But where's this place, and is that where he took Jen?" Emily studied the background for clues.

"There's another set of photos in the next folder."

Emily opened them and revealed a woman in a uniform. "Is she a waitress? I can't make out the logo on her blouse."

"Look at her face. It's the same woman that was in the other photos."

"She really does look a lot like Jen." Seeing a close-up, Emily clicked on that, then stared at the photo for several moments. "I think I've seen her before…but years ago."

"A former classmate? Neighbor?"

"No. But it'll come to me."

"Send those files to this computer right now," he said, giving her an e-mail address. "They'll do whatever it takes to get an ID."

Emily did as he asked, then returned her attention to the photo of the woman tied to the chair. "Look outside the little window behind her. Those are the bluffs. Judging from the angle, I'll bet anything that this photo was taken on the Woods property." She glanced through the cabin's two small windows, comparing. "But not from here."

"The wall behind her is unfinished. It looks like a shed," Jonas said.

"The only other outbuildings I remember on the Woods ranch are farther east of the house. I've only seen their roofs from atop the bluffs, like with this cabin, so I can't give you any more details."

"We don't know for sure where Jen is," he said, thinking out loud. "These photos are of someone else, apparently taken years ago. Now that Grant lives alone, he might have a special place in his home where he takes women. Let's go check the main house first. If we don't find anything there, we'll keep going."

"And if he's at home?"

"Then that'll make my day, but it won't do much for his."

"Sam's truck is right outside. We'll need to borrow it," she said, closing up the laptop and tucking it under her arm.

Jonas hurried outside and peered in the cab. "The keys are in here. Let's go."

"What about the sheriff's department?" she added, climbing in the passenger side and placing the computer on the floor.

"They should be on the way," he answered, knowing the Brotherhood would alert them.

The route north had several sharp corners and side roads, most circling orchards, and fields that had once been cultivated with corn and alfalfa. They took the most traveled route. As Grant's home became visible in the distance, Jonas's cell phone rang.

He listened for a moment, then closed it up with one hand.

"The woman who looks like Jen is Tina Gonzales. Her last employment on record goes back a decade. She worked as a housekeeper for a local service that had dozens of clients."

"That's why I remember her," Emily responded, the memory clear in her mind now. "She cleaned for the Woods family for a while. I'd be at the bus stop and see her turning off the highway in her old VW bug. What happened to her?"

"She disappeared April 28, ten years ago."

"My mom went missing on May 1, ten years ago," Emily said in a shaky voice. "Do you think…"

"Don't speculate, Em. Not now," he said quietly. "Take it one moment at a time."

Chapter Nineteen

Spotting a stretch of split-rail fencing that appeared to be in a bad state of repair, Jonas glanced over at her. "Where are the outbuildings from this location?"

"We'll have to go by the house, then turn east," she said.

"Good. I wanted to check the residence first, anyway. But we need to plan our approach carefully. Grant could be watching for us from the second-floor windows." It took him only a second to make up his mind. "Hang on. We'll make a road of our own."

A moment later, he swerved the truck and crashed through the old wooden rails, cutting across the field, now overgrown with weeds. Jonas eased off the accelerator as they fishtailed on the soft earth. Quickly regaining control, he steered toward the grounds surrounding the solitary ranch house, on the alert for gunfire.

A white pickup was parked at the rear of the building. Jonas kept a sharp eye on the windows facing south, but there was no sign of movement, and their approach went unchallenged. He pulled up a hundred feet from the house.

The rear entrance, leading into a kitchen, was open, the screen door swinging gently in the breeze.

"That tends to indicate he rushed out of there, but can we trust it?" Emily asked.

"No. Grant's other truck might be parked on the north side, out of view, so we can't lower our guard. Just in case he's still here, I'm going in alone," Jonas said, stepping out on the driver's side, but leaving the engine running. "Get behind the wheel and be ready to pull up to the house fast, or drive off, depending on how things go." Not giving her a chance to argue, he moved forward in a crouch to check out the white pickup.

She slid behind the steering wheel, and watched Jonas circle around the building, not taking the bait of an open door. Seconds dragged by, then a minute, and more.

Five minutes later, he came out the kitchen door, holding a black box, and motioned for her to drive over.

Emily did so, then moved back to the passenger side as he jumped in behind the wheel. "Nobody was home, and there was no basement or secret room," he said, handing her the box. "I found this under a bed when I was looking around. Open it while I head to the outbuildings, but don't touch what's inside, at least not directly. If you have to move stuff around, use my penlight," he added, passing it to her.

"There are more photos of Tina here." Emily jiggled the box to see what lay beneath, and inhaled sharply as a pair of broken, retro-style women's glasses came into view. "These are my mom's."

"How can you be sure?"

"She loved those red frames with the large lenses—even when dad teased her and insisted she get rid of them. Look at the way the temple's glued together. She'd broken them, and the model had been discontinued, yet she refused to part with those glasses."

As they drove away from the house, down the tree-lined lane, he pointed. "Roofs ahead."

Slowing to a crawl, he inched the truck around a corner lined with brush taller than the top of the pickup. Stopping, he backed up several feet, then parked at an angle, blocking the road. "If he's here, he must have heard us coming. Driving into such a narrow field of fire makes no sense to me so we'll leave the truck here and go in on foot."

He took the lead as they ducked into the brush to the left, then circled around the buildings. When they drew closer, he could see a large shed and a barn with sliding doors, one open far enough to reveal horse stalls within. Both structures were painted the traditional barn red, but were fading badly. It looked as if no one had done any major upkeep on them for years.

"To my knowledge, Grant sold all the horses after his mother and father died. He has, or had, a few head of cattle, but the good grazing land is farther north and east."

They stayed still for a while, listening, but heard only the rattling of a loose piece of corrugated metal from one of the roofs.

"Let's move in," Jonas finally whispered.

They approached the shed, using a stack of moldy, yellow-brown hay to shield their approach. The wooden building was empty except for a rusted out stock tank lying on its side. The wallboards on the inside had never been painted, and were gray and worn where the elements had taken their toll. Cobwebs, many of them coated with dust, suggested that no one had been in here for months—years perhaps.

"Barn next," he said, staying low.

The shed provided them with cover, and they were able to dash across the gap between buildings. They circled around the barn, which was in much better shape, then entered silently through a rear door.

Empty horse stalls lined both sides of the building, and there was a low stack of good alfalfa hay along the center. It was obvious that this building was still in use.

As Jonas walked down the line, Emily opened the door to the first stall and stepped inside.

"There's fresh hay scattered all over the floor here, but no obvious sign of an animal. I don't see a feeder or water container, either. What about the other stalls?" she asked.

He came back to join her. "The other stalls are clear, and relatively clean and empty."

"The fresh bedding must be here for a reason. Maybe the animal's outside." Emily walked to the paddock area next to the barn and looked around. "There are no animals tracks leading out here. Come to think of it, there are no tracks at all."

"We should at least be able to see ones belonging to whoever maintained this stall. Looks like someone's been careful to rub out their tracks," Jonas said. Heading back into the barn, he looked around. "That window," he said, pointing to the loft above them. "It's like the one in the photo."

Emily moved toward the center of the stall to get a better look, and as she did, heard her footsteps—something unexpected on the thin layer of alfalfa.

"Hollow," she mouthed, gesturing beneath her.

He drew his weapon and motioned for her to step back. On one knee, and using silent, short strokes, he brushed aside the green leaves and stalks, uncovering what lay beneath—a thick wooden trapdoor held shut with a metal bar.

Staying to one side of the opening, he slipped out the metal bar, then pulled the trapdoor open. A wooden ladder led down into a small room.

He took a quick glance inside, then jumped down. Muffled cries rose in the air the second he landed.

"It's okay. It's okay," Jonas said quickly.

Her heart in her throat, Emily rushed to the opening. The stench of blood and fear overwhelmed the wood-lined enclosure. As light penetrated the tiny room, she saw Jen, alive and cowering in the far corner. Her mouth had been taped shut and her hands tied.

Emily scrambled down the ladder, and while Jonas cut the cords, helped Jen remove the duct tape from her mouth.

"He told me he wouldn't kill me. That he'd be careful this time," she said, fighting back tears. "I don't know what he meant. He's crazy. He told me that I belonged to him now."

Emily helped the woman stand while Jonas phoned for help. "Do you know where Grant went?" Emily asked her.

"He said he had two more loose ends to tie up before he came back," she said between sobs.

"Did he say what they were?" Emily pressed, forcing her to concentrate.

"Sam. He said Sam and I had betrayed him. And there was someone else with a strange name."

"Dinétsoh?" Emily asked.

"Yeah, that was him."

As they helped Jen out of the barn and into the sun, they heard sirens coming closer.

"Here come the deputies," Emily said gently. "They've been searching for you. You'll need to tell them your story."

"Don't go!" she begged in a panicked voice.

"You're safe now," Jonas said, "but there's someone else who needs our attention."

"Should I call Preston?" Emily asked, reaching into her pocket for the notebook page.

Jonas nodded. "Update him and stay with Ms. Caldwell while I move the pickup for the deputies and give them Sam's laptop." He whispered the last part so Jen wouldn't hear.

MOMENTS LATER EMILY and Jonas were under way. "We're going after Grant?" she asked him.

He nodded. "He's the one who caused your father's death and tried to track down Dinétsoh—the only witness to his crime. He also set the traps that would have put you out of the picture if you hadn't been careful."

"But where do we look for him?"

"If Grant goes out the main roads, north and west, he'll get caught by my people or the deputies, and there are no roads leading east beyond the stable. What we need to do is cover the other possibility—him heading south in his truck. He probably thinks Jen is well hidden, so if he wants to avoid prison, he'll go back to Sam's cabin to clean up the evidence. Then he'll make one last attempt to find Dinétsoh before somebody else does."

Jonas considered the new picture forming in his mind. "I think Grant saw the signs Dinétsoh left behind before we did, and didn't erase them, hoping an experienced tracker like me would come along. Dinétsoh is a hard man to track, and Grant probably didn't have the skills necessary."

"What if Dinétsoh's passed on?" she managed to ask in a thin voice.

"Even if he has, Grant will need to find the body and make sure there's nothing left to incriminate him, like a dying man's note."

"Then it stands to reason that Grant will head back to the mine, the only hiding place left he hasn't checked out completely. Do you think Dinétsoh stayed in the cave? What we saw might have been a false trail. He could have gone into another tunnel inside that mine."

"It's possible," Jonas answered, wishing he could tell Emily about Fire Rock Hollow. But it had always been need-to-know only. Even *he* didn't know its exact location. All he knew was that Dinétsoh had been replenishing supplies there, and if those had included medical items, there was still hope they'd find him alive.

"What if the police are at Sam's when we get there?" she asked as they raced down the road toward his cabin.

"They haven't had enough time. The cruiser we saw back there at Grant's was the first on the scene. Their priority was the hostage, and manpower's limited. That's why we have to move fast. This will be our last shot at Grant. In a few hours, law enforcement will be all over the place, and the press won't be far behind. If we don't catch Woods now, he'll go into hiding and it'll take years to track him down again."

WHEN THEY REACHED THE cabin, no police were about, but they discovered Grant's big tan pickup among the trees, hidden from view. No one was inside the vehicle, but they could see tracks leading toward the bluffs.

Sam's body lay on the ground where he'd fallen, but his pockets had been turned out. Grant had obviously searched him for any damning evidence.

While Jonas grabbed Sam's rifle, Emily went back to the pickup and retrieved the flashlight she'd seen in the glove compartment. They set out at a brisk pace, following Grant's tracks. As they hurried along, Jonas made a quick cell call, speaking in Navajo.

"Phoning for more backup?" Emily asked, struggling to keep up.

Jonas nodded, calling her attention to the ground. "Grant's moving fast. Notice the distance between his strides? He's followed our old trail to the partially collapsed mine exit we used to escape."

"Do you think he'll be hiding close by?" Emily whispered.

"Yeah. I don't think he knows exactly where to go next. My guess is that he was hoping we'd show up so he could ambush us and force us to lead him to Dinétsoh. Stay close to cover."

With danger near, she watched Jonas turn into the trained warrior he was—muscles tight, reflexes sharp. His work as a member of the Brotherhood gave him purpose and direction. He needed that as much as he needed air to breathe.

In that way, they weren't so different from each other. She wanted security, true enough, but she, too, needed challenges. They added an extra sweetness to life. That's why she'd chosen to become an innkeeper, a job that varied every single day, and why she'd fallen in love with Jonas. Her heart had known her true needs long before she had.

As she picked her way along the rocky slopes, she stumbled. Emily grabbed on to the side of a big boulder and steadied herself.

"Are you okay?" Jonas asked, glancing back at her.

"Yeah, but can we take a break for a moment?" she panted, trying to catch her breath.

He nodded, slowly taking in their surroundings, searching for any sign of movement or a hiding place. It was midafternoon and the rocky bluffs, facing north, had recesses now in shadow.

As Jonas studied the tracks, he saw that Grant had stopped beside the trail next to a distinctive flat-topped rock two feet tall. "Dirt's been scattered over this rock. You can see where sand's been scooped up from the ground and spread in a thin layer on top."

Jonas brushed it clear with his hand, and studied the marking beneath. "An *X* has been carved into the surface."

She drew closer and ran her fingers over it. "This isn't an *X*. It's the Roman numeral ten. I can feel the serifs at the ends, those little lines that finish the letter." She drew in a breath. "This is it!"

"What?"

"Remember my father's note? The starting point of the map was Law Rock. My father told me once that the ten commandments were the blueprint for civilized society. He said that Moses's tablet was the bedrock—the foundation for all modern laws."

"Law Rock," Jonas repeated with a nod. "Grant obviously thought it meant something, so he tried to cover it up."

Emily reached into her jeans pocket and pulled out the note her father had left. "I've kept this with me, hoping to make sense of it eventually," she said, handing it to him.

"'Two hundred forty degrees, three hundred yards, one hundred sixty degrees, fifty yards, and twenty up,'" he read, then took out his GPS, switched it to compass mode and placed it on the X. "Two hundred and forty degrees is west-southwest. I think this is going to take us either directly to the mine or very close to it."

"Let's follow Dad's directions. If we get any indication that Grant is here with us, we can switch our course."

"I was hoping you'd say that," Jonas said, flashing her a grin. "We go southwest, farther back along the bluffs. And stay sharp. Landmarks don't move, but bad guys do."

"Give me the compass, and I'll step it off," she volunteered. "You can keep watch better than I can."

The direction of travel took them toward the bluffs, but after passing a small canyon, they ended up facing a sheer wall of stone.

"Where to next?" he asked.

"One hundred sixty degrees south-southeast. The heading seems to lead to that narrow draw we just walked past." She paced it off, and the route took them into a ten-foot-wide gap between the opposing walls of the cliff.

Turning in a half circle, Jonas spotted a faint trail of black rocks scattered down a steep slope of loose rubble, then a dark opening at the top into the side of the cliff. The narrow canyon itself, in the shape of an upside-down U, continued on around to the west.

They'd started to climb, moving slowly, when suddenly a shot rang out from somewhere just outside the cliffs. Jonas yanked Emily flat, and together they slid down the slope on their stomachs. His body blocked hers from direct fire as bullets whined up the draw and ricocheted off the hard surfaces.

They jumped behind a big rock and Jonas brought Sam's rifle to his shoulder. It was only a .22, but it outranged his Beretta and could take out a man with a well-placed hit.

"Woods!" Jonas called, looking down the sights for a shot. "It's over. Deputies are closing in from the north, and they'll find our location from my GPS. Give it up. The Caldwell woman is still alive. There's no reason for anyone else to die today."

When two more shots rang out in response, he pinpointed Grant's location.

"I know where he is and I'm going after him," Jonas told Emily. "But I'm going to need you to cover me." He handed her the rifle. "No recoil, and you've got ten rounds. All you have to do is line up the front and rear sights and pull the trigger. Shell casings will eject out the side, but don't let that distract you."

"I've fired a .22 rifle before. Are you going to sneak around the back way?" she asked.

"Yeah, I'm going to outflank him. He's between those two big rocks. The one on the left has a bump on the top—see it?"

She nodded.

"Just make him keep his head down, like you did before with the pistol."

"All right," she said, hoping they could finally finish what they'd started. "Be careful!"

"Always. And don't worry. Just give me two shots to make him duck."

She fired, and Jonas dived ten feet to a stunted juniper, using it for concealment. Crawling away, he was soon out of Emily's sight.

As he moved off toward the other opening in the U-shaped canyon, pistol in hand, Jonas focused solely on his target. This was what he did best. Nothing would stop him now.

Chapter Twenty

Jonas crouched low and headed toward his target, ready and eager to meet his adversary head-on. As he remembered all the times Woods had threatened Emily with those close calls, a silent rage burned through him.

He shook free of the emotion and fixed his thoughts on the job ahead. Nothing to excess. Not even anger. In times like this, skill and training had to take precedence.

His approach from Grant's right flank was so silent that the man had no idea what was going on. Woods, who'd moved several feet closer to Emily, was on his belly in a shallow draw, positioned too low to see anyone coming up on either flank until the person was right on him.

Emily fired another shot. It was lined up correctly, but high, and whined over Grant's head.

Jonas heard the man curse, then saw him reach into his jacket pocket. As Grant tried to reload, bullets spilled out onto the ground.

Making the most of the opportunity, Jonas jammed his pistol into its holster and shot forward, jumping on his opponent and knocking him away from his rifle. They rolled on the ground, but Grant kicked free, and hurled himself back at Jonas, flailing his fists like a madman.

Jonas punched him in the nose, putting all his weight behind the blow. Woods screamed and stumbled back, his eyes wild with rage.

Jonas had fought many men before, and knew desperation when he saw it. His opponent would never give up, not until he was unconscious, or dead.

Woods jumped up on a rock, then reached down into his boot, pulling a knife. Leaping to the ground again, he began to circle Jonas, swinging the blade back and forth. "I'm going to gut you like a fish," he sneered, his bloodied face twisted in rage.

Jonas faked a move to the left, then kicked out. The blow caught Grant above his heart, spinning him around. He fell hard onto his chest, his arms pinned beneath him.

When he didn't jump back up, Jonas expected a trick and kept his distance, avoiding Grant's feet. But Woods wasn't moving at all and his breathing was shallow. Blood seeped out onto the ground from beneath his torso.

It took Jonas only a second to realize the man had fallen on his own knife. Approaching carefully, he rolled Grant over, and stared into his fading eyes. The blade was hilt-deep in his chest.

Hearing footsteps, Jonas spun around, drawing his pistol, then saw Emily, her rifle aimed straight at the fallen man. Jonas put away his weapon and reached for his cell phone.

"You," Grant whispered, seeing Emily.

"Don't talk," she said, keeping the rifle aimed at him as Jonas phoned in their location and asked for a medical team.

"A helicopter will take fifteen minutes minimum, and a four-wheel drive vehicle even longer. You'll have to hang on, Woods," Jonas announced after he ended the call.

"Doesn't matter…I'm finished." He laughed bitterly, then coughed.

"We need to pull out the knife," Emily said, glancing at Jonas. "Don't we?"

"No. The bleeding would only get worse. There's nothing we can do with a wound like this."

Emily looked back at Grant. "All this for my land? But why? You've already got more than I'll ever have."

"Still don't know?" he asked, his voice growing faint.

Taking a raspy breath, he continued. "This…your mother's fault…caught me digging hole for Tina. Started screaming… had to shut her up. Hit her with…shovel. Both buried…under concrete."

"Where her hobby room was going to go," Emily exclaimed, suddenly understanding. "Then you parked Mom's car by the bus station so we'd think she'd walked out on us." Emily struggled against the anger that threatened to overwhelm her. All those years of wondering if she'd somehow been to blame. So many sleepless nights and so many tears… As she stared at the man who'd taken the irreplaceable from her, all she felt was contempt.

"When you found out that we were building the inn, you knew Dad and I would tear up that concrete and find the bodies. That's why you killed him, and tried everything you could to force me to stop construction. When that didn't work, I had to be the next to die." Tears streamed down her face. "You miserable…"

"Not my fault," he said, his voice fading to a whisper. "Tried to buy you out. Couldn't kill you… Paid Sam to shoot… But you showed up…alive."

Emily stared at him in disgust. "To think I felt sorry for you once," she said, then turned away.

Jonas came up beside her. "Make up for some of what you've done," he said to Grant. "Tell us where Dinétsoh is."

"Shot him… He ran," Grant answered, his voice a faint rasp. "Was in the car…saw me. Had to die, too. Hid somewhere…out here. Took your father's maps…looked…never found…." Grant coughed, and after a struggle, focused on her. "Found…turquoise key." His chest heaved, then he grew still and the life faded from his eyes.

Touching the dead went against everything Navajo, but

Jonas did what had to be done. Crouching, he felt the pulse point at Grant's neck. "He's gone."

A shudder ripped through Emily and tears streamed down her face. "All these years of not knowing, but hoping…" She swallowed hard, trying to come to grips with the torrent of emotions inside her.

"You have answers—and justice," Jonas murmured, looking down at Grant's body.

She nodded slowly. "Then why don't I feel any better?"

He gathered her against him and stroked her hair gently. "The peace you want can't come until you release the past. But life's opening new doors for you. Walk through and see what you find."

His words revived her spirit and, filled with new courage, she stepped out of his embrace. "We have to go. Someone else is counting on us. Dinétsoh."

"The key Grant mentioned—we have to find it," Jonas said.

"Let me do it." Crouching by the body, Emily searched Grant's pockets. A moment later, she pulled out a key carved from blue-green turquoise and held it up.

Jonas took it from her and gazed at the polished stone in awe. "This is the stuff of legends. To actually see it…"

The key was hand-carved, designed with exquisite attention to detail. Images of warriors inlaid in silver on the upper part gave it almost a life of its own. The blade itself had only two ridges and an unusual looking notch at the end.

"I don't think this is meant to work in the same way modern keys do—to insert in a lock and apply torque to open. The stone would break off if you did that," Jonas said slowly.

"Where does it fit then? A key's function is to open *something*."

"I think we'll find the answer in the mine," he said. "There's something I haven't told you. Dinétsoh and your father shared a secret…."

Seeing Jonas struggle to come to terms with something, she

took his hand and pressed it to her heart. "My father died guarding your tribe's secrets. You can count on me to do the same."

"I believe you," he replied, holding her gaze. After a heart-beat, he continued. "There's a hiding place somewhere in the bluffs," he said, telling her about Fire Rock Hollow. "The cave is said to be a death trap without the key. Dinétsoh was its guardian. The question is, without the key, was he able to make it inside? And if so, was there enough in the refuge to sustain him?"

They hiked back to the opening indicated in her father's note, then climbed down an old mine entrance. As before, the walls and ceiling had been shored up in places with big, heavy timbers, but the darkness was nearly absolute once they moved away from the opening.

This time they had more than just Jonas's penlight to help guide their way, but the flashlight she'd taken from Sam's pickup didn't help as much as she'd hoped. The batteries were obviously old, and the beam was yellow and narrowly focused.

Seeing her trembling, Jonas took her hand in his. "Is it the darkness that scares you?"

She nodded. "It's a reminder of what the future holds for me if I do lose my sight. But it's more than that, too. Down here everything closes in on you. It's like being buried alive. I don't know how miners survive it."

"Mother Earth herself gives them the confidence they need. To them, the tunnels are a way to make a living—life, if you will," he said, leading her into a section they hadn't been in before. "And, of course, they bring big lanterns."

The mine shafts angled only slightly, constructed to follow the seams of coal. Eventually they came across the same natural cave opening they'd found that morning, but from another direction. Jonas crouched down and studied the rock floor with his penlight.

"Now that I have more light, I can see that Dinétsoh's footsteps leading back out were meant to mislead. He came back out, then reversed himself and walked back in, stepping on his exit tracks very carefully."

"Walking backward." Emily nodded. "So he's in the cave somewhere."

Jonas nodded. "Or he went this way, then found another way out. We'll go in to search, but be extremely careful what you touch in case he left more signs of passage."

"I'll need to keep my hand on the rock wall to guide myself, but I'll keep my touch light."

"If you feel anything unusual, let me know. And don't make any snap judgments or take a side passage without checking first. Tribal hiding places are often guarded by traps or pits meant for enemies."

They entered the tall cavern, moving slowly upslope, listening, but the only sound was the hollow echo of their own passage. As they walked along, the height of the cave shortened gradually, putting the roof within reach.

Emily fought back the waves of panic that swept over her. Trying to divert her thoughts, she focused on the earthy scent inside the cave, and noted the places on the walls that felt damp to the touch.

Long tree roots from water-hungry plants had penetrated deep. Some of the hardiest roots dangled like ropes from above, and along the upper walls. Others had dried and fallen to the floor, leaving hundreds of shallow curved and twisting recesses in the walls, much like worm holes.

"We need more light. I can't see anything clearly anymore," Jonas said in frustration. Sam's flashlight had grown ever dimmer, so they basically had only his penlight.

Relying on her other senses, which had sharpened now that her vision was nearly useless, Emily ran her hands over the walls, feeling, searching, using a featherlight touch. Suddenly she stopped.

"There's an indentation here in the rock. It doesn't feel like the others. It's almost key shaped."

Using the penlight, he came over and studied it. "You're right." Taking the turquoise key from his pocket, he slipped it into the crevice and waited, but nothing happened.

Emily suddenly yelped as something brushed the side of her face. "Where did that come from?" She stepped away from what looked like a root that had come loose from the low roof and dangled down. "I thought it was a spider—or worse."

Jonas studied it for a moment. "It's not a branch. It's a rope." Making a split-second decision, he gave it a gentle tug.

Suddenly a deep rumble shook the cave. A thin layer of dust rose from the rocks and a small portion of the wall shuddered open, revealing a doorway.

Beyond, an elderly man wrapped in a wool blanket sat on the cave floor, facing them. He raised his hand, directing the beam of a small flashlight into their faces. "About time you got here."

Chapter Twenty-One

As Jonas stepped into the cavernous room, he saw it contained cardboard boxes of MREs, meals ready to eat. There were also water bottles and other emergency supplies.

"Uncle, I'm sorry for the delay," he said with an answering smile. "I'm glad to find you well."

"Fire Rock Hollow served its purpose," the old Navajo answered. "But getting here was...difficult."

"It's a very long way from the highway, and more so for someone who's wounded," Emily said. Dinétsoh's hair was grayer, but he was still strong—inside and out.

"The air bags saved my life when we were run off the road, but my friend wasn't as lucky," he said, giving her a look filled with sadness. "I'd just managed to free myself from the wreckage when Woods drove up. But instead of helping, he opened fire. I didn't have time to search for my friend's cell phone. All I could do was grab the briefcase and run. I knew Fire Rock Hollow was my only chance, but along the way, I dropped the key. That made getting in trickier, and without it, getting back out was impossible—a security precaution I designed myself."

"You were taking a huge chance. Wouldn't it have been better to hide in the mine tunnels?" Emily asked.

He shook his head. "This was the safest place for the bearer bonds." He aimed his flashlight at the briefcase leaning against the wall of the cave. "What I still don't understand is how Woods found out about them."

"He *didn't* know about them. He had different reasons for his crimes," Jonas said, and explained.

As they spoke, Emily took a few steps toward an inner, adjoining chamber.

"Don't go any farther, niece," Dinétsoh told Emily firmly. "No one except the guardian of Fire Rock Hollow can see all the secrets this cave holds." He looked at Jonas and added, "That will be you, if you accept the charge."

"It will be an honor," Jonas stated, then helped the old man to his feet. "Allow us to help you out of here, Uncle. It's time for you to greet Sun once again."

THE NEXT WEEK PASSED quickly. Grant's two victims were removed from beneath the concrete pad, and Emily was able to lay her mother to rest in a grave next to her husband's.

In the brightness of the morning, Emily watched as the final roof truss for her new inn was lifted into place. The whispers of the past were fading as the future waited to be born.

Seeing a familiar pickup coming up the drive, she stepped forward and waited as Jonas pulled in. "Good morning," she called in greeting.

"I see things are right on schedule."

She nodded and smiled. "And I have more good news. My doctor called this morning. A new gene therapy is scheduled for clinical trials. It shows a lot of promise, and I've been selected to participate. There are no guarantees, but these last few weeks I've learned to take life as it comes. I'm ready for this."

They stood side by side and watched as the workers began to attach the truss with nails and metal plates. "It's time for us to go," he said softly. "Others are waiting."

"I know," she said, and, walking around the truck, climbed into the cab.

As they drove west, toward the reservation, Emily's heart was racing. All Jonas had told her about today was that she'd be asked to take an oath to keep Fire Rock Hollow a secret, then honored for her service to the tribe. She'd pressed him repeatedly for more of an answer, but he refused to tell her anything else.

The trip led them south of the San Juan River and onto tribal land. The relentless march of time inevitably brought progress in its wake, but in the Navajo Nation, change came slowly. Though where they lived was dry and desolate looking in many places, the tribe had managed to hold on to what was important—the hearts and minds of their people. The future here held nothing but promise.

They drove past a chapter house, then turned down a dirt road leading to a hogan at the base of a low hill. White smoke drifted out of the hole in the center of the roof, and Emily could smell the scent of burning piñon pine.

Jonas parked fifty feet from the traditionally built six-sided log stucture, and helped her out of the pickup. "When we go inside, remember that women sit on the north side, to your right. I'll go to the left."

"What else should I do?"

"You'll know as things unfold."

"But—" By then, he'd already gone ahead to hold open the blanket entrance for her, which faced the east, toward the rising sun.

As they stepped inside the small, nearly circular hogan, she saw Dinétsoh sitting on the west side, behind the central fire pit. Two Navajo men were at his sides, one wearing the white headband of a *hataalii,* a medicine man. The men greeted Jonas with a nod, then gestured for her to take a seat on the sheepskin rug.

Emily sat and waited.

"Yáat'ééh," Dinétsoh said in greeting. "I want to do a song of blessing for both of you, a *hozonji.* It'll bring you luck and restore harmony."

"Thank you, Uncle," she answered.

He took a deep breath and began the Sing, accompanied by a gourd rattle and the steady rhythm of a ceremonial drum. The Sing's mesmeric quality echoed with power and the rich cultural history of the Navajo people.

When he was finished, Dinétsoh asked Emily to take an oath insuring she'd protect tribal secrets. After she finished, he continued. "You've completed what your father set out to do, and have done us a great service. You're now *Bik'is*—a special friend."

He placed a small carving before her. "This is a token of our friendship, something you can use to call us should you ever need help. Your friend," he said, nodding to Jonas, "suggested its form."

She accepted the small, dark-colored fetish and studied it closely, running her fingertips over the artifact. The animal figure had been beautifully crafted out of coal. "Can you tell me what it symbolizes?" she asked.

"The heroes in our stories often had mentors," Dinétsoh explained. "That's Pocket Gopher. He was able to see through the darkness, and went where others could not go. In our creation stories, Pocket Gopher's help spelled the difference between victory and defeat."

Emily smiled, realizing her special connection to the fetish. "Thank you," she whispered, touched by the gift and the care they'd shown in selecting it.

"If you feed the fetish pollen, Pocket Gopher will stay strong and aid you in whatever battles you face."

"I'll take good care of it, Uncle, and keep it with me always," Emily answered.

"Now I'll say a special prayer to Gila Monster, who can see into the future and knows everything."

Dinétsoh's song reverberated with a different kind of strength this time, filling the hogan with an energy that could be felt but not seen.

When he finished, the old Navajo looked at each of them.

"I have something to say to both of you. The path of long life and happiness is sweeter when walked in pairs. But to walk in beauty, you have to be willing to let your heart lead you. Go now and remember what I've said."

Jonas stepped outside with her. "I'd like to take you to a place that's special to me. It's in the sacred mountains west of here," he said as they went to his truck. "Will you come with me now?"

"You can take me anywhere you want," she answered, then gave him a slow, mischievous smile.

His eyes lit up with a fire that was impossible for her to mistake. "Remember those words, *sawe.*"

He drove north to the main highway, and forty minutes later, they reached the piñon-covered foothills of the Carrizo Mountains.

Once at the top of the rise, he invited her to join him outside. The reservation stretched out below them as far as the eye could see.

"This is the home of my people. I'm connected to this land, and it to me." He cupped her face in his hands and gazed at her. "You're part of me, too. With you, I'm finally complete. *Ayóó ninshné*—I love you. Share my world, Em, and let me be part of yours."

"You already are. *Ayóó ninshné,*" she whispered, as his mouth closed over hers.

*Fan favorite Leslie Kelly is bringing her readers
a fantasy so scandalous, we're calling it FORBIDDEN!*

*Look for
PLAY WITH ME*

Available February 2010 from Harlequin® Blaze™

"AREN'T YOU GOING to say 'Fly me' or at least 'Welcome aboard'?"

Amanda Bauer didn't. The softly muttered word that actually came out of her mouth was a lot less welcoming. And had fewer letters. Four, to be exact.

The man shook his head and tsked. "Not exactly the friendly skies. Haven't caught the spirit yet this morning?"

"Make one more airline-slogan crack and you'll be walking to Chicago," she said.

He nodded once, then pushed his sunglasses onto the top of his tousled hair. The move revealed blue eyes that matched the sky above. And yeah. They were twinkling. Damn it.

"Understood. Just, uh, promise me you'll say 'Coffee, tea or me' at least once, okay? Please?"

Amanda tried to glare, but that twinkle sucked the annoyance right out of her.

Coffee and tea they had, and he was welcome to them. But her? Well, she'd never even considered making a move on a customer before. Talk about unprofessional.

And yet...

Something inside her suddenly wanted to take a chance, to be a little outrageous.

How long since she had done indecent things—or

decent ones, for that matter—with a sexy man? She hadn't had time for a lunch date, much less the kind of lust-fest she'd enjoyed in her younger years. The kind that lasted for entire weekends and involved not leaving a bed except to grab the kind of sensuous food that could be smeared onto—and eaten off—someone else's hot, naked, sweat-tinged body.

She closed her eyes, her hand clenching tight on the railing. Her heart fluttered in her chest and she tried to make herself move.

Was she really considering this? She had no idea if he was actually attracted to her or just an irrepressible flirt. Yet something inside was telling her to take a shot with this man.

It was crazy. Something she'd never considered. Yet right now, at this moment, she was definitely considering it. If he was available...could she do it? Seduce a stranger. Have an anonymous fling, like something out of a blue movie on late-night cable?

She didn't know. All she knew was that the flight to Chicago was a short one, so she had to decide quickly. And as she put her foot on the bottom step and began to climb up, Amanda suddenly had to wonder if she was about to embark on the ride of her life.

Look for
PLAY WITH ME
by Leslie Kelly
Available February 2010

REQUEST YOUR FREE BOOKS!

2 FREE NOVELS PLUS 2 FREE GIFTS!

◆ HARLEQUIN®

INTRIGUE®

Breathtaking Romantic Suspense

HII0

HARLEQUIN
Ambassadors

Want to share your passion for reading Harlequin® Books?

Become a Harlequin Ambassador!

Harlequin Ambassadors are a group of passionate and well-connected readers who are willing to share their joy of reading Harlequin® books with family and friends.

You'll be sent all the tools you need to spark great conversation, including free books!

All we ask is that you share the romance with your friends and family!

You'll also be invited to have a say in new book ideas and exchange opinions with women just like you!

To see if you qualify* to be a Harlequin Ambassador, please visit
www.HarlequinAmbassadors.com.

*Please note that not everyone who applies to be a Harlequin Ambassador will qualify. For more information please visit www.HarlequinAmbassadors.com.

Thank you for your participation.